A FAMILY AFFAIR: THE CABIN

MARY CAMPISI

MARY CAMPISI BOOKS, LLC

Copyright 2017 by Mary Campisi

A Family Affair: The Cabin is a work of fiction. Names, characters, and situations are all products of the author's imagination and any resemblance to real persons, locales, or events are purely coincidental. This book is copyright protected. If you're reading this book and did not purchase it, or it was not purchased for your use, then please purchase your own copy. Thank you for respecting the hard work of this author.

All rights reserved.

No part of this book may be reproduced in any form or by any electronic or mechanical means, including information storage and retrieval systems, without written permission from the author, except for the use of brief quotations in a book review.

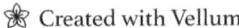 Created with Vellum

INTRODUCTION

He's lost his fortune... She's nursing a broken heart...When fate steps in, will love prevail?

Pete Finnegan had it all—money, power, status, a future wife, until he lost everything in one huge financial "gamble." Now he's back in his hometown of Magdalena, trying to figure out what to do with his life. When he's offered a job fixing up a cabin one hundred miles away, he jumps at the opportunity. Peace and solitude in the woods away from busybodies and do-gooders is exactly what he needs to contemplate his future.

But Pete doesn't expect to find a beautiful woman staying at the cabin.

Elissa Cerdi has escaped to the Blacksworth cabin to heal her broken heart. As Gloria Blacksworth's former caregiver, she's agreed to honor the dead woman's last request by mailing letters to select residents of Magdalena. When Elissa meets Pete, she doesn't know he has ties to Magdalena, and she certainly doesn't know the final letter she plans to mail could destroy his father.

Pete and Elissa are both in need of healing and maybe that's why they agree to pretend nothing exists but what's inside the cabin. But they can't remain there forever. Eventually, the past will resurface and then they'll have to decide if what they shared in the cabin is worth fighting for...

Truth in Lies Series:
  Book One: *A Family Affair*
  Book Two: *A Family Affair: Spring*
  Book Three: *A Family Affair: Summer*
  Book Four: *A Family Affair: Fall*
  Book Five: *A Family Affair: Christmas*, a novella
  Book Six: *A Family Affair: Winter*
  Book Seven: *A Family Affair: The Promise*
  Book Eight: *A Family Affair: The Secret*
  Book Nine: *A Family Affair: The Wish*
  Book Ten: *A Family Affair: The Gift*
  Book Eleven: *A Family Affair: The Weddings*, a novella
  Book Twelve: *A Family Affair: The Cabin*, a novella
  Book Thirteen: *A Family Affair: The Return*
  Book Fourteen: *A Family Affair: The Choice*
  Book Fifteen: *A Family Affair: The Proposal*
  Book Sixteen: *A Family Affair: Bonus Scenes*
  Book Seventeen: *A Family Affair: The Homecoming*
  Book Eighteen: *A Family Affair: The Decision*
  Book Nineteen: *A Family Affair: The Journey*
  Book Twenty: *A Family Affair: The List*
  Meals From Magdalena, A Family Affair Cookbook

Thank you for your interest in *A Family Affair: The Cabin*. If you'd like to be notified of my new releases, please sign up at my website: http://www.marycampisi.com

To Danielle—Firstborn. Shining star. One-of-a-kind. Admired and much loved.

You are all of the above and so much more! Continue to follow your own path, stay true to yourself, and watch your dreams unfold. Your mama is cheering you on!

1

People said spring was a sign of rebirth and renewal. A time to clean up and clean out—rooms, closets, gutters, the past. Especially the past. But was that really true? Christine Desantro studied the sun-drenched roads as her husband navigated the SUV from one winding curve to the next. Soon, they would reach the cabin and the final reminder of her father's secret past.

She'd believed in him, trusted in his honesty and ability to protect her from the harshness of the world. How could she have known he would be the one to deceive her, crush her heart, and leave her with a sadness she would carry deep in her soul for the rest of her life?

There would never be a good time to return to the cabin, not when memories of betrayal clung to the walls and deceit stretched over the chenille bedspread. For fourteen years, they'd all believed this was where Charles Blacksworth sought refuge each month from the demands of running a powerhouse investment firm. It had been nothing more than a grand lie, one that had threatened to destroy her, but ended in her redemption. If not for the lie, she'd never have ventured to the cabin and found her way to Magdalena and the Desantros. She would not have met Miriam, or Lily, or Nate, and she would not have opened her heart to them and found love and a sense of belonging.

The pain and anger of those days were hard to recall, as was the intense dislike for the man who would become her husband. Those emotions seemed almost implausible, as though they belonged to someone else's life, certainly not hers. She and Nate shared a love and commitment built on a foundation of trust and respect. But there had been a time when life had been very different, and she feared visiting the cabin would dredge up the old feelings she'd had about the Desantro family, including Nate.

"Are you sure you want to do this?"

Nate's voice broke through her thoughts, his tone soothing and serious. He'd once vowed he'd never let anyone or anything harm her, including her mother. But what about the memories living inside her head? What about the past life in Chicago he would never really understand? She'd had a mother who believed net worth had a direct correlation to self-worth, and a father who maintained a facade that bore no resemblance to what lay in his heart. How could they not have left scars?

She'd postponed this trip as long as she could, citing one excuse after another: pregnancy, a second child, the holidays, Uncle Harry's birthday. Nate had been patient, but when the new year came, his resolution to sell the cabin came with it.

"Babe? Tell me what you're thinking." He reached for her hand, squeezed.

Christine wished she were back in Magdalena with the girls and the new color-coded recipe notebook Nate had given her last week. It was a compilation of Desantro recipes with easy-to-follow steps that he'd assured her could *not* be ruined. He dubbed them "Christine-proof" and while some wives might take issue with their husband's insinuation that they were horrible cooks, she found his attempt to rectify her lack of culinary skills endearing. And that's why at this very moment she wished she were home, attempting the "Christine-proof" version of aglio olio with angel hair so she could surprise him with dinner. Instead, they were winding along country roads toward the place that had been yet another piece to the mystery of her father. "I don't want to be doing this—" she turned in her seat to face Nate "—but if I have to, I'm glad you're with me."

"I'm always here for you, no matter what." His expression grew fierce, the grooves around his mouth deep. "I hate that you have to go through this. I'd have come here myself, but Harry gave me a bunch of crap about seeing the place one last time so you could have closure."

"Uncle Harry said that?" She smiled at the thought of her uncle spouting off bits and pieces about living right and finding an authentic path. Who would have thought the man who lived for trips to his favorite restaurant and the perfection of his golf swing would change so much? "He's becoming a real philosopher, isn't he? And a mind reader, too." He was definitely right about the closure part. *Get rid of the baggage, Chrissy girl*, he'd said. *If you don't, it will turn into regret and sink you.*

Nate shrugged, his lips pulling into a grudging smile. "The man has almost as many sayings as Pop. I'm beginning to wonder if he isn't going to be the next Godfather of Magdalena."

"Imagine that?" She laughed, but the idea wasn't as far-fetched as it sounded. The town admired Uncle Harry, and not only that, they listened to him.

"Yeah, imagine Harry turning into Pop." He slid her a glance, his dark eyes filled with humor. "Think we should add high-tops and jogging pants to your uncle's wardrobe?"

"Now that would be a sight."

They spent the next several minutes reworking Uncle Harry's wardrobe to include T-shirts with sports team logos, baseball caps, and running jackets—using materials like cashmere, gabardine, and pinpoint cotton. Of course, he'd have to learn the art of making the perfect pizzelle, but Lily would help with that, and Pop could teach him how to read his "audience" when telling a story.

"You know what Harry's biggest challenge would be, don't you?"

She raised a brow. "Keeping the cuss words in his head?"

That made him laugh. "Nope. That's second. The old boy's biggest challenge would be swapping out those designer duds. Not sure he could do that, even if the fabric was high-end. T-shirts and sweats just aren't his style."

"Unless he's exercising. Then he's all about comfort and performance gear." She clasped her husband's hand, leaned back in the seat. "Thanks for trying to take my mind off of what we're doing."

"Who? Me?" He shrugged. "I'm just the driver."

"You're my center, Nathan Desantro." She lifted his hand, kissed it. "You keep me focused and steady, and you give me strength to make the difficult choices." Another kiss. "Thank you."

He nodded. "We're a good team. Some days I feel like we've been together forever. And then there are others, where it seems like just yesterday that you showed up at my mother's door looking for Lily."

"You've learned patience since then."

The grin he gave her said he agreed. "Yeah, well, I was pretty rough around the edges back then. Uncivilized, I think you called me?" The grin spread. "But you didn't seem to mind."

"Because I saw the real man behind the gruff exterior, the gentle one who would do anything to protect his family."

"You saw a lot more than I wanted you to see." He sighed and shook his head. "And once you got inside my head, you camped out and wouldn't leave."

"I kind of like knowing what's going on up there. Very entertaining."

The scowl came next. "I'm sure it is."

Christine laughed and squeezed his hand. "Probably almost as entertaining as knowing what's rambling around in mine."

His lips twitched. "No man will ever admit to knowing what's going on in a woman's head."

The comfortable bantering continued and made Christine almost forget what lay ahead. No doubt, that was her husband's plan, one she should have noticed if her words rang true and she always knew what was going on in his head. She liked to think she did, but with a man like Nate Desantro, a person never really knew. What she did know was that she had his love, his trust, and his commitment, and she didn't need more than that.

Nate rounded another bend and the cabin came into view: a bit older, a bit shabbier, but pretty much as she remembered it. Her husband eased the SUV up the gravel drive, stopped several feet from the wide-slatted, wooden door, and let out a low whistle.

"So, this is the place. Pete's going to have his work cut out for him." He scanned the broken window, the sunken front steps, the birch tree. "Good thing he's got nowhere to be."

Nate was talking about Pete Finnegan, Jack Finnegan's West Coast son, the one who'd returned to Magdalena a month ago under a cloud of questions and mystery. Some said his departure from California where he'd worked as some kind of real estate guru had more to do with a woman and less to do with the change of pace he'd said he needed, while others insisted family drove him home, maybe even the desire *for* a family, as in rekindling with an old girlfriend. Whatever the reason, Pete Finnegan didn't comment one way or the other, his blue eyes intense, his tanned face serious. He was handsome in a rugged blue-jeans-flannel-shirt way; a man who spoke less than Nate, which made the town all the more curious to find out his story. Christine climbed out of the SUV and followed her husband to the front door. "You still have no idea why he's back?"

"Nope." He fit the key in the lock, jiggled it back and forth a few times before pushing open the door. "And don't start asking around." Nate glanced over his shoulder and raised a brow. "No inquiries to Bree Kinkaid either. All that woman needs is a whiff of something and she's on the hunt."

Christine stared at her husband's back as he made his way into the cabin. "Doubtful. She's too busy planning her wedding right now to care about a little bit of gossip."

Nate laughed. "If you think that, then you don't know Bree Kinkaid. That woman will be sniffing out stories when she's walking down the aisle." He reached for her hand, smiled. "Forget about Bree, okay? Let's take a look around."

She'd prefer to continue talking about Bree's antics and the new man in town's motives for being there—anything but dealing with the memories inside the cabin. The place reeked of desolation and emptiness. The blue-and-cream-plaid couch with the matching cushions was a bit more faded, the small coffee table and hurricane lamp covered in dust. Her gaze landed on the blue ceramic ashtray, an interesting choice for a man who did not smoke. Why was it here? What did it mean?

"Christine?" Nate squeezed her hand, said in a gentle voice, "Let's just get through this place and then we'll hit the road. If you see anything you want, let me know. We can box it up and take it with us now or set the stuff in a pile for Pete. He's got a big truck, so that won't be a problem."

Her husband knew how to calm her, knew also how to burrow inside her heart and let her know he'd always be there for her. She nodded, touched his jaw. "Thank you." She glanced at the blue ashtray again, pointed to it. "I know this sounds silly, but I think I want the ashtray. Dad never smoked but he bought my mother beautiful ones when they were first married."

"Okay, an ashtray it is." Nate snatched up the ashtray and tucked it under his arm. "Anything else from the living room? Books? The lamp?"

She shook her head. "It was probably a waste to come here. Pete could have boxed up the whole place and I wouldn't have missed a thing. I don't know why we didn't just ask him to do that."

"Because you need closure, and coming here one last time is important. It doesn't matter that your father moved to Magdalena at some point and abandoned this place. What matters and what you should think about is that he *did* live here, and not only that, the reason he came here at all was to rest and rejuvenate. Think about that and not what happened after."

"You almost sound like you're championing his cause."

He raised a brow, the brackets on either side of his mouth deep. "Hardly, but I can appreciate his intentions, even though he couldn't carry them through. The guy had a helluva lot to deal with every month."

"You mean my mother?"

Those dark eyes turned black. "Yeah. Your mother."

Nate would never forgive or forget the pain she'd caused them, and he didn't like talking about that time in their lives, but he never tried to stop Christine if she felt the need to bring it up, usually to work out an issue. "I wish my father had told me how unhappy he was." She moved to the bathroom, flicked on the light and took in the old double-faucet sink, the rust around the chrome fixtures, the porcelain tub with claw feet. Her gaze narrowed on the cracked bar of soap sitting in a white plastic tray: the same soap she'd seen the first time she came.

Nothing had changed, and yet everything had changed.

"How was your father supposed to let you know he was unhappy? You were his daughter; you worshipped him. He couldn't tell you he was living a lie and kept another family you didn't know existed." He sighed, dragged a hand along his jaw. "I get it. If Anna and Joy lost faith in me, I couldn't stand to see the disappointment on their faces, and they haven't been walking this earth very long. Your father had twenty-some years with you."

"I don't know whether to be annoyed or moved that you're trying to justify his actions."

He shrugged. "I'm trying to be logical about it." He paused, added, "Speaking as a father. Of course, if he hadn't put himself in that position, we wouldn't be having this discussion."

"True." She studied him, the dark eyes, the firm set of his lips, the furrowed brow. Nate Desantro was an unbending man who believed in honor and integrity, and she loved him for it, even when those values got in the way of things like forgiveness and second chances. "If he hadn't done what he did, we wouldn't be standing here now, would we?"

Nate stroked her cheek, his voice rough. "Nope."

"Exactly." She leaned on tiptoe, placed a soft kiss on his lips. "There's nothing but dust and sadness in this place. I don't know why I thought it might be different."

"Now you know." He took her hand, led her down the hall toward the bedroom. "Let's check out the rest of the place and then we can get started on Pete's list. Maybe we can find a little restaurant in the next town on our way home." He slung an arm around her shoulders and smiled down at her. "Okay?"

She nodded, walked with him into the bedroom, her gaze settling on the chenille spread. It brought back too many reminders of the lies that had lived below the surface of her family's existence, pretending normal, stretching into other areas, making them doubt and lose trust. Christine turned away, moved toward the chest of drawers, pulled one open. Nothing but a lint brush and a comb. The second drawer revealed two folded undershirts and a pair of white athletic socks. She picked up the socks, traced the ribbing, wondered if he'd started wearing these when he added flannel to his wardrobe.

"Christine?"

There was so much she'd never know about her father.

"Christine!"

She swung around, noticed the mattress against the wall, the chenille spread and cream sheets bunched on top of it, the pillows tossed on a chair in the corner. The bed had been stripped of everything but the box spring. "Nate? What are you doing?"

The dread in those dark eyes turned darker, his voice deeper. "I thought I'd make it easier for Pete to paint. It's so damn small in here I was worried he wouldn't have room for a stepstool, let alone a ladder. I figured I'd move the bed to the other side of the room and flip the mattress while I was at it. My mother was always big on mattress rotation." He held out a hand, tossed several white envelopes onto the box spring. "But I'll bet she never found anything like these."

2

There were six envelopes. Yellowed, the front of each scrawled with names Nate recognized; Gloria, Harry, Christine, Lily, Miriam, and Nate. He'd bet the new addition on his house that Charles Blacksworth had written the letters, and he'd bet there was some damnable incriminating evidence inside.

Or a confession. One just as bad as the other.

Why did people feel the need to unburden themselves by confessing to all sorts of secrets and missteps so those left behind had to deal with the fallout? He scanned the envelope addressed to him. What could Charles Blacksworth possibly have to say to him? Had he asked for forgiveness, or had he taken a more philosophical approach and tossed out terms like *karma, finding one's path*, and *divine intervention*? And Christine? How did a father justify keeping a second family? He did not even want to think about what might be in the letter to Lily or his mother.

"My father wrote these." Christine's voice held a note of awe and reverence, as if the man had drifted from the sky and planted the envelopes under the mattress. She reached for the one addressed to her, fingered the lettering. "I wonder how long they've been here."

That sounded an awful lot like hope sprinkled with the need to believe the guy might have been about to do the right thing. Yeah, a lot of people were *about* to do the right thing, but never actually *did*. It was hard to figure out a man like Charles Blacksworth because people like him were run by fear, duty, and the inability to make a choice.

And they were most often influenced by others, say, a wife like Gloria Blacksworth. Nate couldn't control what was in those letters, but he sure as hell could control what happened to them. "There's only one way to find out." His wife's gaze sparked with understanding—and fear. Once the words inside the envelopes escaped, they'd settle in her brain, infiltrate memories, and create doubts that would never go away. "It's up to you, Christine. You can read them, or you can burn the damn things."

She eyed the letters as though they might lunge at her. "These could have been one of the last things he touched." Sadness smothered her next words, squeezed his heart. "Maybe he planned to return here and mail them. Who knows?" More sadness, this time mixed with despair. "We have to find out when he wrote them." Tears rimmed her eyes. "It could have been shortly after Lily was born. Maybe he was torn between returning to his life in Chicago and staying in Magdalena, and these letters tell that story." She sniffed twice, swiped at her cheeks. "Or maybe he wrote them right before he died. What if he came here to clear his head and write what was in his heart?"

Nate kept his expression bland, his breathing even. What she really meant on the last one was what if the guy suddenly developed a conscience and wanted to do the right thing by everyone. He blew out a quiet breath, forced a nod. "Yeah, who knows?" He'd have to see the damn words before he gave the guy credit for making a tough choice because it was the right thing to do.

"Will you read them to me? It'll be easier to handle if you're reading them."

"Sure." He scooped up the letters and made his way to the other side of the bed. "Come here, babe." Nate pulled her into his arms, held her against him. "No matter what's in these envelopes, we'll get through it together." He stroked her hair, murmured, "I'll always be here for you."

"I know," she mumbled against his chest. "Thank you."

"Come on." He pulled away, took her hand. "Let's go sit in the living room." He'd known Christine would have to deal with memories of the cabin, but he'd never thought there'd be a land mine waiting for them in the form of six letters. Damn Charles Blacksworth for once again messing with their lives.

When they were settled on the couch, Christine rested her head on his chest, blew out a tiny breath, and said, "Okay. I'm ready."

He pulled her closer, kissed the top of her head. Why couldn't Charles and Gloria have been like normal parents, loved their daughter, put her needs ahead of their wants? Why did those two have to be so screwed up? It wasn't the money that made them that way, but something deeper, more fractured, and Nate would do anything to protect his wife from more grief at the hands of those two. He eased the first letter from the envelope. It was addressed to Gloria. "Here we go."

DEAR GLORIA:

I have thought of sending this letter so many times, but I could never quite bring myself to do it. Why was that? Fear? Worry? Weakness? I've spent most of my life shouldering the responsibilities of running a company and providing for my family, and while the weight has been heavy at times, I've never regretted it. Nor have I regretted marrying you. We share a daughter who has given me more joy than I ever thought possible. I hope one day she will find her own path to happiness. We have not been the best role models for Christine and I wonder if our issues have kept her from finding someone who values her, someone she can love. Connor Pendleton is not that man. Love and marriage must be about more than joining families to build empires. Pendleton is more interested in our daughter's portfolio than her thoughts. We must take partial responsibility for that. I'm referring to the deficiencies in our own relationship. Surely, you know they exist. Don't you?

When my sister died, I realized how precious life is, and how very unpredictable. I would never hurt you—not intentionally—and I will always care about you, but I can't go on pretending happiness and contentment in our marriage and neither should you. We may share a home and a name, but "we" died years ago. I see 2 choices: continue as we have been, living as strangers, or divorce and begin a new life. I choose life. I hope you will, too. When I return to Chicago, we'll meet with Thurman Jacobs and discuss what needs to be done. I'd like us to tell Christine together.

Gloria, please know I will take care of you and make sure you want for nothing. You must wonder why I've chosen to tell you of my decision to end our marriage in a letter instead of face to face. I wonder this myself and yet I know it is the only way I can release the words I've carried in my soul for too many years.

We are still young enough for a second chance at happiness. Let's take it.

I'll see you in a few days and then we'll talk.
Always,
Charles

. . .

NATE FOLDED THE LETTER, returned it to its envelope. There'd been some powerful words in that letter, but there'd been no date, and for all anyone knew, they were only words. Had the man had any intention of putting action behind them? Hard to tell and unless the other letters gave a clue, they'd never know. "Should I read another one?"

"I want to hear them all, Nate. Don't stop until you've finished the last one."

"What's the rush?" Reading the letter to Gloria made him squeamish. He'd never been big on too much emotion, good or bad, and reading about a dead man's intentions was pretty much on the high end of emotional overload—and not in a good way. "Wouldn't you rather read one or two a day? Kind of ease into your father's news so you can think about what he has to say?"

"No."

He waited for her to elaborate, and when she didn't, he picked up the next envelope. This one was addressed to her. Nate set it aside and picked up the letter to Harry. Of all the tasks they'd planned to do at the cabin, reading her dead father's undelivered letters wasn't even on the list of possibilities.

HARRY:
I'm writing this letter because I need your help and I'm not sure I can get the words out any other way. I've been living a lie—a big one—and I can't do it any longer. I don't want to do it any longer.

I'm in love with another woman. Her name is Miriam and I met her shortly after Ellie died when I started coming to the cabin every month. Ellie's death made me realize a lot of things, especially my own mortality and the fleetingness of life. Miriam and I have been together fourteen years and we share a child named Lily. Yes, I really did just write that. Lily is pure and innocent and when I'm in Magdalena, I'm alive. Really alive. It's my life in Chicago that has become the lie, but it's been a lie since long before I met Miriam.

What I'm about to write is a deep, painful secret I've kept hidden for years. I'm telling you now because I need your help with Christine. This secret destroyed my marriage even though it took years to acknowledge it. Gloria had an affair before Christine was born. I can see the shock on your face, probably as great as mine was. Shortly after I learned of the affair, she found out she was pregnant. I moved out of the bedroom, distanced myself, and planned to divorce her if the child didn't look like me. But there's no denying Christine is a Blacksworth from the hair to the eyes. For that, I am grateful.

I loved Gloria but I was so immersed in work and reaching the goals Dad set for me that I didn't take time to be a good husband. I didn't know how to be one. Something shriveled inside me when I found out about the affair and once Christine was born, my hope and love went into her. Gloria will not take this easily but I AM leaving. I plan to move to Magdalena and will visit Chicago four days a month to conduct business. I'm stepping down as CEO of the company and would like you to consider a larger role. You have a lot of talent but you get in your own way.

Maybe one day you can visit Magdalena. I think you'd like it. The people are a good, honest bunch. I'd like you to meet Miriam and my daughter, Lily, and I would love for Christine to meet them one day, too, but how would that ever happen? It will have to remain an unfulfilled wish.

You've never been one to judge—thank you for that. I'm going to need all the help and support I can get and I know I can count on you. I'll be home in a few days and we'll discuss this in greater detail.

Charlie

MY SWEET LILY:

Do you know how much Daddy loves you??
I love you...
more than three scoops of cherry chip ice cream.
more than Mom's banana nut bread.
more than snow angels on a starry night.
more than ten flannel shirts!
more than my fuzzy slippers and you know how I love those!
more than our walks in the woods.
more than sitting by the Christmas tree drinking hot chocolate with tiny marshmallows.
Bundle all of these together and I love you MORE!!
You make my heart smile every time I look at you. You're growing up, Lily girl, and next month we'll drive to the stables and check out the horses. Your birthday will be here before we know it and what happens when you turn 14? You're going to ride a horse!!
I'll have to get extra film for my camera so I can take a lot of pictures. Do you think 10 rolls will be enough? When we're together again, we'll count the days until your birthday and your very first horse ride!!
I'm sending you a big hug—bigger than the whole state of New York.
Love,
Dad

NATE PLACED a kiss on the top of her head, and whispered, "Are you sure you want me to keep going?"

"Yes, let's just get through this."

Dear Miriam:
I am writing this letter to you from the cabin. I needed clarity and if I were surrounded by you and Lily, I might never put pen to

these words and they very much need to be written. You, of anyone, know the struggles I've battled for the past fourteen years. I should have acted on what lived in my heart years ago, but I couldn't. Fear and duty kept me prisoner. And let us not forget the weakness that owned my soul and rendered me incapable of making the difficult choice.

We never spoke of it, because what good would it have done other than to remind us of my life in Chicago—a life without you and Lily? Do you know how much I missed you both when I was there? How I longed for Lily's smile? Counted the days until we could spend a quiet evening together? Last month, Lily called me a king. "You are the king of our world," she said. "You will never let anyone hurt us. Mr. King." She'd smiled, so bright and pure, beaming with honesty and an admiration I did not deserve.

Lily's words have given me the courage to write this letter. Our daughter will never be accepted into mainstream society as relevant or essential, but she possesses more wisdom than anyone I've ever met. You and I have spent the past fourteen years making a life out of four days a month. Imagine if that number were reversed—if I spent four days a month in Chicago and the rest in Magdalena with you and Lily? Could you tolerate me? I have dreamed this when I've permitted myself to do so, and what are dreams if we have no hope of turning them into reality? I want a life with you, Miriam, a real life, not a patchwork of days and "X's" on a calendar and promises of "next time." Nate won't be happy about it. In fact, I expect he'll try to interfere, but I'm hopeful he'll change his mind about me when he realizes I'm here to stay. I don't blame him for disliking me. He's an honorable man who loves his family. Maybe one day he'll find the right woman and start a family of his own.

I've written a letter to Gloria informing her of my plans. By the time I arrive in Chicago, she'll have the news and knowing Gloria, the battle will have begun. What can she hope to win? More money? The house? She can have those. What she's lost and what she'll never have again is my heart. That belongs to you. I must go gently with Christine, and maybe one day she'll understand and perhaps even accept my decision.

Divorce is never easy on a child and it's more difficult when other parties instill venom and lies in the telling with disregard for the child, concerning themselves only with retribution, no matter the cost. My brother will help me with Christine and watch over her when I am in Magdalena. Harry is a good man with a kind heart who loves Christine as though she were his own.

Next month we'll have much to discuss! It will take some time to get everything in place, but I hope to have the new "schedule" set by Lily's birthday. Won't that be a great present? Not as much fun as a horse ride, but I think she'll be happy.

Finally, we will move forward with the next chapter of our lives, and we'll do it together. I can't believe I'm actually writing this. I love you, Miriam, with every part of me, and I look forward to spending the rest of my life with you.

Love Always,
Charlie

NATE:

This is not an easy letter to write. I've watched your hatred toward me grow each year, and I can't say I wouldn't feel the same if I were in your position. Giving your mother and Lily four days a month isn't enough, is it? I could argue that memories have been built on far less, but we both know that's a coward's answer, just as we both know I'm a coward. They deserve far more than I've given them, and it has been my inability to make the difficult choice that has hurt everyone.

You have no reason to believe what I'm about to write, nor am I asking you to, for what good are words without actions? But I vow on my love for my daughters, Christine and Lily, that I will make this right. I can't undo the past fourteen years or the animosity you feel toward me, but I can and do choose to spend the rest of my life with my family—here, in Magdalena.

I don't know if you will ever be able to forgive me, or if I even have the right to ask, but know this—I will be living in Magdalena by Lily's birthday and I will watch her ride her very first horse. Do you think we can coexist? Is that possible? Maybe years from now, when you have a wife and children, you will be able to open your heart and look at things differently.

Until then,
Charles

NATE FOLDED the letter and set it aside. "Your father was right about looking at things differently once I had a wife and children. If he could only see us now..."

"I think he'd be very proud to call you a son-in-law."

He wasn't sure about that, but it certainly would have been interesting. "Okay, this last letter is for you."

DEAR CHRISTINE:

Life is short. A breath of air and then it's gone. When we lost Aunt Ellie to cancer, my whole world shifted. I had believed time was limitless and the people I loved wouldn't die until they'd lived full lives. I thought the same for myself. But when Aunt Ellie died, it was a wakeup call. We didn't have unlimited time, certainly not forever. All we really had was now.

Please don't squander your time and your life on a man like Connor Pendleton. He doesn't deserve you, doesn't appreciate you, and doesn't respect you. Find your own happiness. Take a day off, step away from the computer, look around. Have you wandered into the kitchen lately when you're visiting and smelled Greta's cooking?

Or watched her roll out a pie crust? It's as impressive a feat as choosing a good stock.

I don't want to see you "stuck" in a life you don't want with a man you don't love. Duty is a cruel taskmaster. Do not be governed by it. Our company was built on performance, commitment, and expectation. But to what? Money? Power? Advancement? Your Uncle Harry could not live that life and your grandfather could not accept that.

Do not let others define you. We are all human with weaknesses and frailty, me more than most. My shortcomings are not yours. My failings do not belong to you and are not because of you. There is a whole world outside of Blacksworth and Company Investments. Explore it. Drive to the country. Eat a bowl of beef stew. Look around. Listen. Live your life, not mine, not your mother's, not anyone else's.

I love you, Christine. I have loved you from the moment I saw you and will love you until I draw my last breath.

I will see you soon!
Love,
Dad

NATE FOLDED the last letter and placed it with the others on the couch. He would have rather done three straight days of inventory than read those letters. Too much emotion, too much pain, too much damn speculation and not knowing. His wife's voice sifted through his thoughts, pulled him back.

"He really was going to leave us."

Such sadness, such resignation. Nate cursed the irresponsibility of a man who was supposed to be all about honor and decency. Right. As long as nobody dug too deep, and life didn't get too complicated for him. Then what? He'd straddle the problem, the one *he'd* created and let both sides dangle "You don't know what your father would have done. People say they're going to do things all the time, but how many get around to actually doing it? There's the guy who's going to write a book, or quit the job he hates, or ride cross-country in a motor home. And what about the woman who vows she'll leave the husband who's cheated on her so many times she doesn't count anymore? They all talk big, but when it comes time to act, they can't do it."

The sniff said the tears were coming. "Part of me wants to think he'd make the tough choice and follow his heart, but another part feels...abandoned."

"I know." Charles Blacksworth had abandoned Miriam and Lily, too. Maybe he'd been about to change all of that, who would ever know? "Whatever his plans, they died with him on that icy road."

"It's obvious from a few of the references he made that he wrote the letters shortly before he died."

"True, but we're never going to know if he planned to mail them."

Christine eased her head from his chest, met his gaze. "What other reason would he have to write them?"

Those blue eyes filled with confusion, uncertainty, and a tiny bit of hope. Nate wanted to help her find peace, but her father hadn't made it easy, not with six letters and too many unanswered questions. "People do things for all kinds of reasons. For all we know, writing the letters could have been a way to unburden himself, like going to confession and asking for absolution."

She nodded as though considering this possibility. "I guess." Her gaze landed on the stack of letters. "I'm not sure what to do with them. Would it be better or worse for your mother to know he wanted to marry her and planned to get a divorce? Think of that, Nate. She'd accepted their situation, but can you imagine learning he'd finally found the courage to do what was in his heart and then he died?" Her voice drifted, spilled over him. "I'm not sure I could take learning that about the man I loved."

"*If* he planned to mail them."

"You've got a jaded view of my father, so it makes sense you wouldn't think he'd change. But why couldn't your mother believe he'd gone to the cabin right before he died, wrote the letters, and planned to return the next week to deliver them?"

Was this a trick question? He was a literal guy, so he'd give her a literal answer. "Because it might not be the truth?"

"But we don't know that."

"No, we don't. So, you're saying we should let everyone create their own story with their own ending?"

A tiny nod. "How else will we be able to move on?"

He rubbed his jaw, not liking where this was going. "I've never believed in fairy tales or closing your eyes and pretending something didn't happen. I tend to look at the odds and someone's history, but that's just me. Before you hand out these letters, think about what could happen, positive and negative. If there's more negative, don't do it. Take Harry's letter, deliver it, and you'll destroy the guy. You need to shred the damn thing and be done with it."

"You don't think he'd want to know that my father didn't think of him as a failure, that he believed in him?"

"Hell no!" How could his wife not see the destruction inside the letter? "If Harry reads that, then he'll also read the part about the affair and how your father needed to confide in him. Come on, do you think your uncle will recover from that? It would take him down so fast, there'd be nothing left of the poor guy. Do not tell him. Destroy the damn thing."

She gathered up the letters, her voice all business, as

though they were discussing a balance sheet. "I have to think about it."

"Fine." When she pulled away like this, it was best to leave her alone for a while. "Now how about we pack up that ashtray you've been toting around and get the list going for Pete so we can get out of here?"

"Nate? It's not that I don't trust your judgment; I just need time to think about everything." She placed a hand on his forearm, worked up a smile. "I'd never do anything to hurt Uncle Harry. You've got to trust me on this."

"I do trust you, but a lot of people have been hurt by others trying to do the 'right' thing. Who can say what's right and wrong? I sure as hell can't, and neither can you. All I do know is that I won't stand by and watch Harry's world collapse on top of him."

"I would never wish that on him."

He didn't miss the displeasure in her voice. "I know you'd never intend to hurt him, but do you know how many people say that right before they destroy the other person? Don't be that person, Christine, or you could blow up a whole lot more than your uncle's happiness."

3

Elissa Cerdi believed in love at first sight, happily-ever-after, and the goodness that lived in everyone. Some called her naïve, impractical, even foolish for guarding her beliefs, but she knew what she knew and what she wanted. She'd witnessed her parents' marriage—the love and respect they shared for one another—and had vowed she'd settle for nothing less. People who didn't think true love possible were the naïve ones, or maybe they'd lost the ability to hope. Elissa refused to give up hope because if you didn't have hope, what did you have?

As for finding goodness in others, had she not discovered it in Mrs. Blacksworth when the poor woman's family deserted her? Accused her of horrible deeds the woman could not have committed? How could an only daughter reject her mother, especially one who was dying? Christine hadn't known of Mrs. Blacksworth's illness; that had fallen on Elissa, a weight she'd gladly carried. When the money and fancy lifestyle were stripped away, what else was left but the desire to not die alone, to leave this world with grace and dignity?

Mrs. Blacksworth had not died alone or without the grace

and dignity she so rightly deserved. Elissa would like to think she'd eased the woman's passing. Yes, her employer had demanded she accept a substantial amount of money for the final-wishes favor she wanted Elissa to execute once she was gone. There'd been no need for extra money; Mrs. Blacksworth had paid her well and Elissa would have performed the final-wish favor—deliver the remaining letters from the notebook—without an extra penny. It was the right thing to do in honor of a friend, and Mrs. Gloria Blacksworth had indeed been a friend, a sad one with a broken heart.

Could the family not have understood that the harshness in the woman's words were born of disillusion and heartache rather than cruelty and a desire for vengeance? There was one more letter to deliver and then Elissa would have fulfilled Mrs. Blacksworth's last wishes. She offered a quick prayer for the woman who'd stopped believing in joy and hope long before she drew her last breath. "Holy Mother, I pray Mrs. Blacksworth has found peace and knows the joy and hope that lives in all of us. May you keep us in your prayers and guide us always. Amen." One quick sign of the cross, followed by, "And bless your children, Elissa and Zachary, as they plan their future. Thank you, Oh Holy Mother. Amen."

Prayer helped her stay focused on what mattered in life, like the people she loved. Like Zachary Wintstone. Next week, they'd announce their love and intentions to the rest of the world in a small engagement party at The Presidio. Zachary's parents dined at the upscale restaurant several times a week, and he'd told her they'd insisted the gathering be held there. Elissa would have agreed to anything as long as the man she loved was by her side. She sighed, opened the door to the lobby of the apartment where he lived. Once they married, she'd pack up the tiny place she rented on the other side of town and move in with him. Once she married...

How lucky could one girl be? Zachary Wintstone was handsome. Brilliant. A wonder boy with computers and the world of technology. They'd met in a coffee shop nine months ago. The connection was instant, fierce, all-consuming—just like she knew it would be. Her mother had maintained when the right one came along, Elissa would fall hard and give her whole heart to the man. She'd been right about that, but then, her mother knew about relationships and life.

If only she'd been more open-minded about Mrs. Blacksworth. Why were people with money so often misunderstood and misjudged?

Elissa walked across the lobby, pressed the elevator button, and waited for the ding that would take her to the eighth floor and her future home. Zachary's place had the little extras that welcomed visitors, made them feel at home: the overstuffed pillows, the cylindrical vases stuffed with silk daisies, the bowl of fruit on the kitchen table...even the selection of hand soaps showed a personal touch—so like her fiancé. She smiled at the thought of shopping with him, selecting picture frames for their wedding photos and, later, those of their children. The smile spread when a woman with a baby stroller entered the building. Model-beautiful with long black hair and a body that didn't look like it had seen pregnancy. Was *she* the mother? When the woman reached the elevator, Elissa peeked inside the stroller, took in the black curls and pink skin of the baby. "Girl or boy?"

The woman's green eyes softened, her voice a rush of wonder. "A boy."

Only a mother had that particular glow and spoke with such reverence. Elissa had witnessed it in her own mother when the youngest child was born. One day, she would know such a feeling. "What's his name?"

"Christopher." Another rush of emotion swirled through the woman's voice. "He'll be three months old next week."

"He's beautiful." She and Zachary wanted two children, a girl and a boy, the order didn't matter, and the gender didn't either, not really. A healthy baby was all she needed. Elissa studied the newborn, thought of the good fortune and love the child's parents must share.

"Thank you." The woman beamed, growing more beautiful, if that were possible. "He's our own little miracle baby." She pushed aside a lock of dark hair, her eyes misting. "Placenta previa at twelve weeks. We almost lost him. But God and mountains of prayers saw him through." A sniff, a tear swipe, followed by a quick sign of the cross and a glance at Elissa. "Do you have children?"

The elevator dinged open, giving Elissa an extra two seconds to compose herself as the impact of the woman's words hit her. *Placenta previa. Miracle baby.* It took brave people to venture into parenthood, to risk the love and loss of a child. She cleared her throat and said, "We've got a few things to settle before we start a family." *Like an engagement party, a wedding, and a honeymoon.* Elissa held the door open for the woman to maneuver the stroller into the elevator and pressed the button for the eighth floor. "Which floor?"

"Eight, please." A smile spread over the woman's full lips, brought out the dimple on the left side of her cheek. "Children will change your life. You'll never look at your partner or the world the same way again." She met Elissa's gaze, held it. "You'll see."

"I hope so." Elissa glanced at the baby. "You certainly don't look like you've just had a baby." She let out a soft laugh. "I don't even want to think about what I'll look like." Another laugh, followed by a sigh. "My mother says everybody thought she was carrying triplets when she was pregnant with me. That's not what I wanted to hear."

"It's all worth it."

"I know." The truth was, she'd face stretch marks, spider veins, heartburn, and whatever else maternity threw her way for a chance to be a mother. One day soon, she and Zachary would sit down and talk about a timeline for parenthood. After all, if you didn't have a game plan, how were you going to get anything accomplished? Zachary claimed she was too focused on fitting life into a schedule, that most times life had to be lived, not controlled. But why couldn't a person live a *controlled* life? There was nothing wrong with spontaneity, and she subscribed to it every now and again, but she didn't want her existence to be determined by the sun, the stars, and the direction of the wind. Or whatever. She liked order. She needed routine. No surprises, at least not the ones that upended a person's day-to-day existence and spiraled them into a universe that had no center and no direction.

The elevator dinged for the eighth floor, and Elissa held the door open. The woman pushed the stroller onto the plush carpet and waited for Elissa to join her. "Do you live here or are you visiting?"

Now that was a matter of opinion and interpretation. "My fiancé lives here, but I'll move in once we're married."

"Really?" The woman's face lit up. "Mine, too." She hesitated, her cheeks turning a dull rose. "I've only been in Chicago a little while. I'm from Seattle, but when I found out I was pregnant, he wanted me closer. I've got a place a few miles away, but I'm moving in with him soon."

"Congratulations." There was something about this woman that drew Elissa to her, made her want to get to know her better, call her a friend. She didn't seem to know or care that she was beautiful or that others would no doubt stop and stare. That made her more human, and *that* made Elissa curious. "Maybe once we're settled, we could all get together. I'll fix dinner and you could bring your fiancé and the baby. There's plenty of room."

"I'd like that. Thank you." She held out her hand, "I'm Julia."

Elissa shook it. "Elissa."

"Nice to meet you, Elissa. I look forward to meeting your fiancé."

"Same here." Would the man be as gorgeous as she was? Probably. Wasn't that always how it worked? The beautiful people attracted the beautiful people, but if he were as unaware of his attractiveness as Julia was of hers, then he was a rare find. Zachary called Elissa beautiful, but he was blindsided by love because her nose was too long, her cheeks too full, her eyes too far apart, and, of course, what woman didn't think her butt was too big? Only those who thought it was too small, and the universe didn't have many of that type running around. If Zachary analyzed her with the skill he used in his work, he'd notice all her flaws. But he said Elissa's physical appearance was a weak imitation compared to the beauty that rested inside —in her heart, in her soul. Every single time he told her this, she cried.

Julia raised a hand and said, "Until we meet again." Elissa watched as she strolled down the hall, paused seven doors down, pulled out a key and fitted it into the lock. Seconds later, she and Christopher disappeared inside Zachary's apartment.

~

THERE COMES a time in a woman's life when she knows the man she loves is lying to her, even as she's hoping with her whole heart that she's wrong. But deep down, she knows she isn't wrong, knows the half-baked stories he's feeding her that make no sense are full of untruths. She can close her eyes and pretend, or she can face the truth and confront him.

Love. What a sad joke.

She'd had so many plans, each one grander and more intricate than the last, all built around hopes and dreams. Elissa had spent the last several hours with timelines and spreadsheets, dropping in dates and events. The date she met Zachary in the coffee shop, the first dinner…the first time they made love. How had any of this been possible? *How had she not known another woman was carrying his child?* When he'd said he had a meeting in Seattle, was he visiting Julia? Maybe they'd had a quiet dinner and spent the night together. Anything was possible. Who knew? Who really knew?

Nobody.

Julia said she had a fiancé. That was another level of incredible. There'd been no reason for her to lie…and there'd been every reason for Zachary to do so. Had he proposed to Julia when he found out she was pregnant? Or had that come later, maybe after the birth? Maybe he'd gotten a two-for-one deal on engagement rings and proposed back to back? Why not? *Sure, why not?* There were so many possibilities and Elissa had suffered through most of them. All she wanted now was to disappear so she'd never have to speak to or about Zachary Wintstone again.

But the Cerdis were made of stronger stuff. Had Great-Grandma Antoinette Cerdi not immigrated with three small children only to lose her husband to pneumonia the next winter? And had that same woman not kept her family fed by gardening, baking bread, and making her own pasta? She'd mended their clothing, accepted hand-me-downs from the neighbors, and never uttered a word of despair. If Great-Grandma Cerdi could stand strong amidst such heartache and grief, then Elissa could do the same...eventually...after she buried her dreams of happily-ever-after and acknowledged that she'd chosen a liar to share her life *and* her heart.

Of course, Zachary wouldn't see it that way. He'd have a tale, just like all the ones he'd been telling her the past year, and if she let herself, she might believe him. Oh, she wanted to turn back the hours to a time when she *did* believe him, when she didn't know what she knew in her heart. But then what? Let the lies ruin her? The second the beautiful Julia entered Zachary's apartment, Elissa sensed the truth; Julia was Zachary's fiancée, too, and Christopher was his baby.

As she lay curled in bed that night, a cold pack pressed to her forehead, her body damp, her stomach raw from emptying it, she knew what Mrs. Blacksworth must have felt like when she learned of her husband's secret life. *I'm so sorry, Mrs. Blacksworth. So sorry you had to go through that.* For twenty-four hours, she ignored Zachary's phone calls and text messages. As the messages grew more frequent, the tone bordered on panic.

Elissa, call me. Where are you? I'm worried about you.

Hey. It's me. I had to go out of town, but I'll be back in the morning. Call me. Pause. *I miss you.* Longer pause. *We've got to talk about the engagement party. Just call me.*

There were five more messages, each more urgent than the last.

I called your parents' house and left a message, but I haven't heard from them. I know how your mom hates missing a phone call, so now I'm really getting worried. Where are you?

And then, *Your sister sent me a text and called me a bastard, said she hoped I burned in hell. What's she talking about? Why would she say that? Elissa?*

Oh, there'd been a lot of panic in that last message. Almost as if he knew she'd figured out his deep, dark secret, but Zachary wasn't one to divulge more than he had to until it was necessary. That's how he'd been able to wheel and deal in the corporate world and hold out for the best offer. He'd once told her he could poker-face it and threaten to walk away, actually walk away, and they'd always call him back and agree to his terms. Always. The way he'd said this made her think he liked toying with people's emotions to see how far he could get and *how much* he could get. Is that what he'd done with Elissa and Julia? Pushed them both to see how far he could get? Well, he'd ended up with two fiancées and a baby.

How could she have been such a fool? Two months ago, when her mother asked why Elissa still hadn't met his parents, she'd found ten reasons, all of them believable, especially to her. But the real reason was probably the most unbelievable and yet most obvious. Zachary already *had* a fiancée and it wasn't Elissa. She'd been so head-over-heels for him that she hadn't questioned or complained about his demand for space, attributing his need for time alone to do his work and the brilliance of that mind she loved so much.

Except the mind she'd loved with such fierceness hadn't been inventing or contemplating anything in the computer world. No, that mind had been inventing more lies and contemplating ways to cheat on two women. How had he done it so well and for so long?

Why did he have to pull her in and make her believe he cared? Her parents wanted her to call Father Patrick for guidance. Her little sister wanted to find someone to "beat the crap out of him." Elissa wasn't going to let someone else confront the man who'd ruined her life and her belief in happily-ever-after, because one day soon she would handle him herself.

That day came two hours after Zachary's last message, the one that said he'd just landed at the airport and was on his way to her apartment. She showered, tossed on jeans and a T-shirt, and pulled her hair in a ponytail.

She'd always looked forward to spending time with her fiancé, anticipated his arrival with such eagerness that in retrospect, it was sickening. How easy it must have been to play with her emotions, as though she didn't matter, as though he could do anything and she'd believe him. Which she did...all the way up to the second where she'd watched Julia and her baby enter his apartment.

Now, everything had changed. Elissa's heart no longer beat for the man who'd promised her love and happiness until they drew their last breath. That heart was bruised, tattered, cold. Empty.

When the doorbell rang, she made her way to the front door, opened it. Zachary Wintstone faced her, his lean runner's body dressed in slacks and a sweater, mouth firm, brown eyes serious. He looked exactly as he had the last time she saw him. Elissa narrowed her gaze, tried to detect a crack in the facade that might let her see his other life—his other family. Same dark curls that reminded her of Julia's baby, same serious expression, same stance. *Same everything.*

If she hadn't decided to surprise him with a visit the other day, how long would it have been before she found out about Julia and Christopher? After the wedding? After their first child? Or would life have continued for years, as it had with Mrs. Blacksworth, until one day the truth leaked out and her world landed on top of her?

"Elissa. Do you know how worried I've been?" Zachary stepped inside, reached for her, but she stepped back.

"Don't."

"What's wrong?" His voice spilled concern. "You look sick. Why didn't you answer my calls? Talk to me. You know you can always talk to me."

A few days ago, she'd believed he was her everything,

believed they would grow old together. "I will always wonder if the lies started before or after you met me."

"What are you talking about?" Confusion and what looked like fear clouded his dark eyes.

She clasped her hands together, planted her feet in a stance that said she could land a solid punch to his jaw if provoked. "If everything about us was built around a lie; can you at least give me a few minutes of truth? I know about Julia." She paused, gauged his reaction: a mix of shock and disbelief. "And Christopher." A decent guy would own up to the subterfuge, apologize, and call it quits. But then, a decent guy wouldn't play house with one woman and have a baby with another. She spotted the exact second his expression changed and the next words out of his mouth weren't warm and fuzzy or apologetic. They were harsh and accusing despite the softness in his tone.

"Were you spying on me?"

"Spying? Of course not. I wanted to surprise you. I thought I'd stop over so we could talk about the party." *The engagement party for the wedding that was supposed to mark the beginning of the rest of our lives.*

"You shouldn't have done that." His voice was so quiet, so unaffected. "We had an understanding."

"An understanding? What, I stay away from your apartment so you can play house with another woman? You told me you needed to think, that you required hours and hours of quiet so you could work on your projects. I believed you." Elissa swiped both hands across her cheeks. *Damn tears.* "I did the math. We must have just started dating when Julia found out she was pregnant. Why didn't you tell me then? Did I not deserve to know? Or, did you think you could have both of us? Two separate families and neither of us knowing about the other?" The tears streamed down her cheeks to her chin, onto her chest.

"Damn you, Zachary, did you think so little of me that you thought I didn't deserve the truth?"

He shook his head. "I couldn't tell you because...I couldn't let you go. *I love you*, Elissa, love you so much it hurts."

She swiped at her face again, blinked hard. "Do not say that."

"But it's true. I love you. You, Elissa Cerdi, and it's you I want to marry." He dragged a hand through his hair, sighed. "Julia and I were together before I met you; nothing serious, just a few laughs and a drink or two."

"I think it was a little more than laughs and drinks."

His jaw tensed but he remained calm. "Okay, we had a thing, but when I headed home after the conference, we were done. I didn't hear from her again until after you and I were getting serious...that's when she told me she was pregnant. I wanted to tell you, and I kept trying to find a time, but I was so damn worried I'd lose you..."

"So you proposed instead?"

"That's not why I proposed." His dark eyes softened. "I proposed because I loved you. And I still do." He moved toward her. "Julia's a great person and I love my son, but she's not the woman I want to spend the rest of my life with...that person is you."

When he talked like that it was hard to tell if he were lying or if he meant what he said. "She called you her fiancé."

Those lips she'd kissed so many times pulled into a gentle smile. "Saying it and wishing it doesn't make it true. She wanted a life with me, but that wasn't going to happen. Do you know why?" His smile deepened. "Because I wanted a life with you; the whole 'happily-ever-after,' babies, and suburbs. With you, Elissa, nobody else."

He sounded so convincing, so honest. A tiny piece of her

believed him. "Why did she have a key to your apartment?" If he could answer that and it made sense...

"She said that was the only way I could see Christopher." The dip in his voice pierced her heart. "He's my child, and no matter how he got here, I love him. I had to do whatever it took to see him and I couldn't tell you, not yet. I'm sorry, but I was so damn afraid of losing you."

There were tears in his eyes, pain in his voice. She inched out her next words. "Have you been sleeping with her?"

"No! God, no."

He answered so quickly and with such force, how could she *not* believe him? And yet, he'd looked away, just for a second, as if gathering his thoughts or maybe hiding something he didn't want her to see. Like the rest of the truth? Could she live her life wondering what he was doing when he wasn't with her? Would she be one of those women who resorted to checking his phone and computer for signs of...what? Another woman? *Another life?* Would she end up like Gloria Blacksworth, estranged from her family, spending her final days with hired help because she'd refused to confront the truth?

Maybe Zachary was in some bizarre way a victim of bad timing and bad choices. But he'd kept it all a secret, living a lie that included another woman and a baby.

"Elissa, baby...I know you have a lot of questions, and I know you're hurt." His voice cracked. "Whatever you want to know, all you have to do is ask. Okay? Anything. I don't want to lose you." He paused, touched her cheek. "I love you."

Those three words gave her the answer she needed. *I love you.* Had he spoken those same words to Julia? Only a fool would believe he hadn't, and only a fool would believe he wasn't lying to her right now. She'd spent her whole life believing in the goodness of others, trusting them to do right, refusing to acknowledge the dark side of human nature.

And look what had happened? She'd believed everything her fiancé told her, no questions, no suspicions, nothing but blind trust and belief in that damn goodness...

"Elissa? I'll tell you whatever you want to know."

Now he would tell her about his double life?

Now he would tell her the other woman was a mistake and the baby was a consequence of that mistake?

Now he would tell her that if she only gave him a chance, he'd worship her, cherish her, never, ever give her reason to doubt him again? He'd earn her trust back and spend the rest of his days proving he loved her.

He would make her happy.

If she only gave him a chance.

Maybe the words would hold true, or maybe they would only be true the moments before and after he spoke them. Maybe when he walked out the door, he would return to his old life, his *other* life.

Who could say? Certainly, she couldn't, but what she *could* say and what she knew deep in her soul was that she couldn't trust him, not anymore. If she couldn't trust him, what future did they have?

None.

She knew that, even as she motioned him into the living room, sat in the rocker her parents had given her when she moved into the apartment, and eased the look-alike notebook she'd created to mimic Mrs. Blacksworth's from the end table. There was pain and sadness in this book, and so much torment. Was it not fitting that Elissa should add her own pain to these pages? She grabbed a pen, opened the notebook to a blank page, and said, "Start talking."

Two hours and twenty-three minutes later, Zachary finished his tale. There were tears with the telling, gasps and long sighs accompanied by folded hands, soft pleas, and a prayer or two.

Elissa observed and jotted down his words like a stenographer in a courtroom, emotion removed. She tried to focus on the details as she wrote: the sound of his voice, the gestures, the pauses. It was as much what he did not say as what he said that mattered. Later, she would piece it all together as she and her mother had when they'd set out quilting squares for a comforter. Once the pieces were in place, she would look for patterns in his words that contained truths and nontruths. The smallest details, when stitched together, often carried the greatest significance.

The outcome didn't matter. Zachary had destroyed their chances of a happily-ever-after the second he began keeping secrets, secrets that supported lies...lies that ruined her belief that love and goodness prevailed...that if you loved someone, it would be enough...that if you led a good life, then fortune would guide you to happiness...

Lies, all of them.

"Elissa?"

She blinked hard, tried to focus as he crossed the room and knelt beside her. When had he started looking so pathetic, so guilty? How had she never noticed this before? Because she'd never looked, never believed there was a reason to doubt.

"Is there more, Zachary?" *Do not let there be more than this.* How much more could there be than his admission that he and Julia shared a child, that he'd struggled these many months with a way to tell Elissa the truth? "If you have any hopes of a life together, you'd better make sure you've told me everything." Look at her, telling her own lies. Hell could freeze over ten times before she'd give him another chance. Still, her words might pull the truth from him.

He placed a hand on her arm, his gaze intense. There'd been a time when she'd gotten lost in that look. "I don't want to hurt you more than I already have."

That sounded like a confession without the confession. "Tell me." *There was more.*

A shrug, a sigh, and then, "I might have left out a few details about my relationship with Julia."

"Details?" She forced her breathing to remain even, her voice calm.

The man who'd broken her heart and was now ripping it apart with *details* continued. "I might have been intimate with her a few times after...after you and I met."

Did he think using a word like *intimate* didn't sound as bad as sex? Like in some way, it was less hurtful? "So, you were having sex with both of us."

"Elissa—"

"Is that everything?" *Dear God, what else could there be?*

He looked away, lowered his voice. "I'm only telling you this because I don't want any more lies between us, okay? You're the one I love, the one I want to marry." Pause. "You are my heart, Elissa Cerdi, my soul."

She pushed aside the words that had once stolen her breath. What were words without meaning behind them? "Tell me the rest, Zachary. Tell me all of it."

Tears shimmered in his dark eyes, slid down his cheeks. "Julia's pregnant again."

4

Pete Finnegan liked the woods, his English pointer, dark ale, and a meal that could be made with one pan. The simple life, his mother called it, and he agreed. But the life he'd left four months ago hadn't been simple, and it certainly hadn't involved woods, an ale, or a simple meal. Nope. That life had been all about glitz, glamour, and keeping his soon-to-be fiancée happy. If he'd taken a deep breath and looked around, he would have seen he didn't belong in a city any longer, no less a city where people were directed and redirected like cattle. Forget names or faces and to hell with common courtesy. Above all, do not make eye contact. No idle chit-chat either. Who cared why the cashier wore a sling on his right arm or the young boy limped. And if the attendant who's been parking the car for two months straight doesn't show up for a week, don't ask. Not. Your. Problem. And it sure as hell wasn't your business.

But Pete had grown up in Magdalena, been surrounded by people who made it their business to know about busted arms, limps, and anything else that involved a town resident. If anybody had turned up missing—with Magdalena's definition of missing, which was unavailable for longer than a two-hour stretch—there'd be a plan of action in place involving a search party headed by the police department *and* volunteers. Residents didn't fool around, especially in the winter, when snow, ice, and frigid temperatures could threaten a person's life.

He'd been gone from Magdalena fifteen years, but he'd never forgotten the closeness of the town, bordering on what he'd called nosy. At twenty, he'd wanted people to stay the hell out of his business. That included his parents, especially his father, but Jack Finnegan wasn't about to sit by and watch his son cause embarrassment to the Finnegan household. Okay, so maybe underage drinking at "Dave's Happy Hour" in Renova hadn't been a good move, and maybe Pete's temper had gotten the best of him, but he'd been twenty friggin' years old. A kid. Did his old man really have to force his hand? *You want to be one of them free spirits, on your own with not a single soul to answer to, huh? You think that's life? You think that's what will happen when you head to California? Huh? Go on, pack up your bag and go, Mr. Unconventional. Go save a tree and grow a ponytail. See where that gets you.*

Pete's mother hadn't wanted him to leave, had told him years later a piece of her heart broke off the day he drove the old jeep out of Magdalena, but he'd been determined to prove his father wrong.

And he had.

Seems he had a talent for spotting run down real estate that could be turned into lucrative property with a little work and a lot of vision. There'd been big payouts. Huge, in fact. By twenty-six, Pete had enough cash to travel the country in a private plane, trade out the jeans for custom suits, buy a place with an ocean-front view, and accumulate more friends than a football stadium. The women came along, too, blonds, brunettes, redheads.

It was a wild time.

It was fun and dangerous, and as the years rolled by, Pete's obsession to be the best consumed him. *That* was the beginning of his downfall. One gigantic, risk-heavy deal, that was more about winning than strategy, failed and stole everything. Gone were the houses, the cars, the vacation spots. The friends. The woman he planned to marry. Heather. She'd trailed her slender hand along his jaw, placed the softest kiss on his mouth, and told him she wasn't equipped to live a life of want and worry, one without money. And then she was gone.

Everybody and everything he'd identified with evaporated in the span of forty-six days. There were no more deals to be made, no boardroom handshakes or late-night drinks. Pete's arrogance and belief that *he could not* fail proved his greatest failure.

He'd just turned thirty-five. For the next four months, he traveled to places like Oregon, Utah, Colorado, stopping long enough to earn a little cash to keep the old truck he'd picked up running. What he'd once earned in minutes with the click of a button would now take him days, and involved mucking stalls, carrying wood, building and staining fences. But he did it; he did it all because the work was honest, the sweat was real, and when he closed his eyes at night, he was too damn tired to think about regrets.

He'd landed in Magdalena last month, driving in the same as he'd driven out…angry, broke, and determined to find a way out of the mess he'd created. Yeah, he'd sure made a name for himself, but one look at the townsfolk told him they thought the stories about his great success out west were more fiction than fact. Who could blame them? When a thirty-five-year-old limps home in an old truck and moves into the room where he grew up, that doesn't spell success.

Nate Desantro had hired him to fix up a cabin and that

meant time alone without questions or judgments. Nothing but woods and solitude. Pete spotted the cabin, pulled the truck off the road onto the gravel driveway. Why was there a car with Illinois license plates parked near the front door? *Illinois? What the hell?* He pushed aside thoughts of his sorry-ass life and hopped out of the truck. If somebody was poking around inside, maybe taking up squatter's rights on property that didn't belong to him, well, Pete was not going to sit by and let it happen. Nate wanted him to get the place ready to sell and that's what he planned to do. After all, he'd given his word and while it might not stand for much out west, in this part of the country, it still meant something.

He made his way to the compact car, peeked inside. Nice and neat, no food wrappers, napkins, scraps of paper...no socks, hats, tennis shoes...nothing but a string of red and gray beads dangling from the rearview mirror. If he had a guess, he'd say the car belonged to a woman and the woman was a neat freak. Pete glanced at the driveway and the grass surrounding the cabin. If the snow were still on the ground, there'd be a better chance of tracking the intruder's comings and goings. But spring had come early and the rains hadn't kicked in like he remembered they used to after a long winter. He tried to open the car door, but it was locked, a sign that the intruder was not only neat, but careful.

Pete reached in his jeans pocket, dug out the key to the cabin, and headed toward the steps. Some people might call the cops if they suspected someone had moved into their vacant place, but not him. He'd rather figure out the lay of the land before he made any quick judgments or took action. It could be a young kid, hitchhiking and down on his luck, or a couple playing house, or an old man who had no place to go and no family. He fit the key in the lock, eased the door open with a creak.

The first thing he noticed was the smell. Not musty air or staleness as he'd anticipated, but blueberries and butter. The next thing he noticed was the orange and green bag on the end of the couch with knitting needles and a skein of yarn poking out. Candles on the coffee table...a pack of matches...

Who the hell was staying here and why? Paperbacks lay stacked on the other end of the couch. He counted seven. A notebook with a rose glued on the cover sat beside them. No television. Imagine that? He guessed life did exist without televisions and remote controls. Pete followed the blueberry-butter smell to the next room, which must serve as a dining area where a single place setting with a knife, two types of forks, and a spoon rested on a wooden table. A bouquet of greenery had been plunked in a water glass and tied with a pink ribbon.

This was definitely a woman's handiwork, which meant the intruder was either a woman on her own, or part of a couple. When Pete reached the kitchen, he found the source of the blueberry-butter scent. Twelve blueberry muffins with sugar-cinnamon crumble tops lined the cooling racks. The dishes were washed and drying on a towel. He moved to the stove, lifted the lid on the large pot, sniffed. How long had it been since he'd eaten a bowl of vegetable soup? Ten years? Longer? He guessed the last time was when he left Magdalena, fifteen years ago. Pete grabbed a spoon from the utensils on the drying towel, dipped it in the soup, and tasted. Just like his mother used to make...

"What are you doing?"

He swung around, spoon in hand, and came face to face with the intruder. A woman. She had chestnut hair, hazel eyes, and lots of curves. A beautiful woman. The most dangerous kind.

"What are you doing?" she repeated, her voice clipped, eyes narrowing on the spoon in his hand.

Pete set the spoon on the counter, rubbed his jaw. "Good job on the soup. You know, I'm wondering the same thing myself. What are *you* doing?"

She yanked out her cell phone, held it up, and spat out, "I'm going to call the police and report you for trespassing."

That was a good one. She was going to report *him*. Pete crossed his arms over his chest and stared her down. "Go ahead. I'm supposed to be here." He gave her the look he'd perfected years ago, the one that made people nervous. Not this one. She kept that hazel gaze trained on him and lied.

"You're trespassing on my property."

Great. A beautiful woman *and* a liar. "You sure about that? I saw the Illinois license plates on the car..." Let her weasel out of that one.

"Is it against the law to have a vacation spot in another state?" She let out the tiniest huff, clutched her phone, and snarled, "You need to leave or I swear, I *will* call the police."

"Uh-huh." Pete scratched his chin, debated his next words. The woman was lying, but why? She appeared to be alone. Was she on the run from someone or something? Did he care? He'd been sent to do a job and all he wanted was a little peace and quiet while he tried to figure out what he was going to do with the rest of his life. A thirty-five-year-old shouldn't have to crawl home and ask for his old room back, but that's what had happened, and it wasn't pleasant. In fact, it sucked, and it was all on him. His old man hadn't said a word, just eyed him up and down, nodded, and tossed a house key his way, reminding him to lock the door when he came and went.

"Mister, do you hear me? This is my place and you have to leave."

Maybe he should tell her the truth, but that seemed too easy. He'd rather let her dig herself deeper before he blew the lies apart. Besides, he was hungry and vegetable soup and a blueberry muffin or two made his stomach rumble. "A man hired me to fix up the place and get it ready to sell."

Those hazel eyes widened. "A man?"

"Yup." He opened a few cupboards, located two bowls, and set them on the counter. "I'm hungry. How about you?"

HIS NAME WAS PETE, no last name given. Elissa thought of making up a name for herself, but decided on the truth. Well, the truth with her name. The other stories she told him were contrived and the look he gave her throughout most of their meal said he knew it. She told him she'd known one of the owners, which was true, and had always wanted to visit, but life had gotten in the way. Again, sort of true. When Mrs. Blacksworth talked about the cabin, Elissa had grown very curious, though not curious enough to ask to visit. But cheating fiancés had a way of driving a person out of town, making her seek safe haven, and a place to think. The cabin in the Catskills was the perfect spot and since she had a key and as far as she'd known, the place was empty, she'd figured why not? What could a few weeks in the woods do but help her gain perspective? She'd been here three days and was just getting comfortable with the night sounds and the creaking floorboards when Pete with no last name showed up.

Did he know Christine and Nate Desantro? Oh, she hoped not. They would not be happy to hear Elissa had invaded their cabin, especially if they found out she'd been the one delivering the letters as per Mrs. Blacksworth's last wishes. And she had another one to deliver, this one headed to Nate Desantro, and it had to do with his long-time employee, Jack Finnegan. She wished she hadn't agreed to deliver the letters, but she'd promised and she couldn't go back on her word to a friend, especially when that friend was dead.

"So, you're not afraid to stay out here all alone?" His gaze narrowed on her. "I took you for a city girl, but...am I wrong?"

What could it hurt to dole out this bit of truth? She nodded, tried not to notice the man's strong jaw, the cleft in his chin, or the blueness of his eyes. Way too handsome. Elissa shifted in her chair. "Chicago born and bred."

"Ah, Chicago. A city girl, for sure."

She shrugged. "I might be a city girl but my parents took us camping every year. Mountains. Fresh water. Hiking trails. Lots of animals..." The memories crept over her, made her smile. "Those were good times."

"Sounds like it." His voice softened for just an instant. "Nothing gives you perspective faster than fresh air and walking trails. It's a one-way trip to peace."

There was a sadness in his voice, filled with what might be regret. She knew the sound of regret, had heard it enough times in her own voice. What was this man's story? He had one, no doubt about it, and she guessed it centered on a wrong choice. A woman? Of course, there would be a woman. Nobody looked like this man and didn't have a woman, or women. Elissa tried not to notice the long, leanness of his body, the muscles, the jeans that hugged his thighs. And that mouth: full lips, perfect for smiling and...kissing. But when he turned his attention on her, those blue eyes zeroing in, his body leaning toward her as though she were the only woman in his world, well, she could see where there could be trouble or fireworks...probably both.

"So." Pete cleared his throat, toyed with his knife. "We've shared a meal and small talk. Guess it's time to own up to what you're doing here because we both know this isn't your place." He waited for her to attempt an objection and when she didn't, he continued, "I know that because the real owners hired me to fix up the place." More throat clearing. "To sell."

Elissa darted a glance at him, wished she hadn't. Those eyes were homing in on her in a hunt for answers. Dang it all, she'd never been good at lies or pretending. When people told her something, she believed them. Why wouldn't she? And if someone asked a question, she answered with honesty. Again, why wouldn't she? It was how she'd been raised, how she wanted to live her life.

And that's why it had been so easy for her ex-fiancé to create a separate life. All he had to do was conjure up a few tales and she'd believed him—even if his answers didn't quite add up. She'd never investigated or questioned because that would have meant doubting the man and doubting their commitment to one another. Once a person did that, there was no going back to a point where you didn't doubt, where you believed with your whole heart.

"Elissa?"

She let out a sigh, planted her hands on the table, and forced herself to look at him. What was the point of faking it? There was no way to erase the past or wish her ex-fiancé had made a different choice. What was done was indeed done. "I came to get away and sort things out." He lifted a brow, waited for her to say more. "I found out my ex-fiancé had another girlfriend, another fiancée, actually...and a baby. Of course, I didn't know about either until I surprised him at his place. I'd always wondered why he didn't want me going there without his okay. No drop-ins or surprises." Her voice dipped. "He said it had to do with needing quiet time to think and create for the tech company he owned, but that was all a lie."

The man across the table rubbed his jaw. "Yeah, I call bullshit on that one. You never suspected he had a woman on the side? Or a baby?"

"No." Why was he looking at her like that? "What? How should I have known?"

"You were planning to marry the guy. How could you *not* know?"

"People lie and some lie very well." She didn't like the look he'd given her, as though it were a deficiency to trust someone. "Do you think you'd be able to tell when a woman's lying, especially one you trust?"

"I'd know."

"Humph. Lucky you. I must be the only fool in the world because I had no idea. If I hadn't decided to go against his wishes and surprise him a week before our engagement party, we'd be working on the wedding invitation list and picking out china patterns."

Pete shook his head. "The guy was a jerk. Did you at least keep the ring?"

"Of course not. I didn't want any reminders of my horrible error in judgment."

"Don't be so hard on yourself. You trusted the guy; nobody can fault you for that."

"Live and learn, right?"

His lips curved into an almost smile. "And don't be so trusting next time."

"Exactly." Elissa raised her wine glass, saluted the air. "Exact-ly." She finished her wine, set the glass on the table with a dull thud. "But now here I am, almost thirty years old, with a detailed list that includes a husband, two children, and a dog by thirty-four, and I'm back to square one."

"Ah..." He nodded his dark head, the almost smile slipping to a real one. "You're one of those list people: make a plan, follow the plan, and don't deviate, not even for a jerk-cheating fiancé."

She frowned, rubbed her forehead. "I don't know how I

missed the signs." A sigh, followed by a bigger sigh. "I learned a lot. Never again."

"Never again what? Never again trust a guy or never again miss the signs that he's a jerk?"

Elissa poured more wine into their glasses. "Both, I think." The realization that she might never trust a man again was sad, but in some ways, comforting. At least, she'd go into future relationships with her eyes wide open: no expectations, no dreams, no hopes of happily-ever-after.

"Trusting the wrong person is a real bitch."

That statement made her perk up. "So, you've got your own battle stories."

"Don't we all?"

"Was it a woman? Did she cheat?" On second thought, maybe it wasn't the woman at all. Her voice dipped. "Did *you*?"

"It wasn't me."

She shouldn't have asked that last question because the look he gave her said he didn't appreciate the accusations or the prodding. "Sorry, it's not my business."

"How about we get the dishes cleaned up and then we'll continue with the twenty-five questions." Before she could answer, he stood and began clearing the bowls and silverware.

Elissa studied him as he carried the dishes to the counter, filled up the sink with sudsy water. This man had a lot of secrets; she could tell by the way his expression changed when they hit on subjects like lying and fiancés. Maybe he'd had a woman who'd cheated and broken his heart, though why anyone would cheat on a man like this was difficult to imagine. Still, it happened, and the why made her curious. Telling a stranger about Zachary wasn't like confessing the sordid truth to her parents, which she'd done the other night through two boxes of tissues. This was like pretending the stranger cared that she'd been hurt, that the dips in his voice wanted to soothe her sadness, and those eyes saw into her soul. So what if it weren't real? She'd thought she had *real* with Zachary and he'd been the grandest pretender of all. Why couldn't she and this man pretend for a little while? They could share their stories and maybe find peace through the telling and a way to get past the pain?

Yes, that was exactly what she wanted to do, and with a bit of coaxing and another glass of wine or two, she might convince the man with the compelling blue eyes that pretending with a stranger was better than pretending with someone you loved.

5
───

How the hell had she gotten him to talk so much? With the exception of the creditors and the banks, he hadn't told anybody about the sorry state of his life. Talk about a cluster, it had been all of that—one grand tsunami, disrupting whatever life he'd thought he'd had, which had pretty much been built with too much money and too many fake friends. Even the girlfriend he'd thought would become his wife had dumped him when the trouble started and the money ran out.

"So, you were in real estate and you bet all your money on a high-risk deal and lost?"

"Pretty much." Hearing the words spill out of the woman's soft lips like she was trying out cuss words was a real eye-opener. Not in a good way. The truth was he'd been so damn arrogant, so full of self-importance and the desire to be number one, that he hadn't thought he *could* fail. The riskier the investment, the better. When the "wins" toppled his competition, it made him more untouchable, more sought after, more "godlike." Only he wasn't, and he'd found that out the hardest way of all—self-destruction. No one questioned the business deals that included acquiring distressed commercial real estate, pumping money into the buildings, and selling them off at a huge profit. There was one particularly high-risk project he should have avoided, but who was going to warn him against it? Nobody warned a king. Not business associates or banks, not friends or a girlfriend. Would he have listened to them if they'd expressed concern about leveraging so much when he already had more than enough?

Of course not. *This deal was personal.* This deal was about who would rule commercial real estate: Pete Finnegan or Marcus Attican, his nemesis and main competition. It was all or nothing and they both knew it. When a person believes he's invincible, he's going to jump off the building, right? Because he's not going to get hurt. Hell, he won't even get a scratch. So, Pete jumped—and fell—hard, fast, and with such force that all he had left after the destruction was a narrow escape from bankruptcy, a disgraced name, and a ton of regret. No business associates, no friends, no Heather.

Pete shared this story with Elissa, all of it, though later he'd wonder why he'd done it. Maybe it was the way she tilted her head and listened with what looked like complete interest, rapture even. Nobody had done that in a long time, unless he'd been talking numbers and bottom line. But Elissa, whose last name he didn't know, acted as if she cared. Or maybe it was just another part of the pretending they'd agreed upon earlier—pretend the outside world didn't exist—just for a little while. He hoped it wasn't that, hoped maybe one person in this screwed-up universe actually cared about what he said.

But who the hell really knew?

"Why didn't you stay in California? I'm sure you could have found something else to do while you built up your business again."

She said it with such sincerity that he told her the truth. "I torched my career so bad I had to come this far to get away from the fallout. Besides, it was time to head back this way." He shrugged, toyed with the frayed edge of his jeans hem. "California didn't feel like home anymore."

"Of course it didn't," she said, her voice soft and comforting. "Home is the only place that feels like home." She paused, her eyes bright. "Unless you find someone to share your life. Then anyplace that person is feels like home."

Pete cleared his throat, looked away. "I guess." Heather had a lot of ideas about what she thought home was, but he doubted they were as simple as "wherever he was." They were wrong for each other on so many levels, and it took his business and his life to explode for him to understand that.

"So, tell me about the place where you grew up."

He slung an arm across the back of the couch and smiled at her. He could get used to the comfortable conversation and the curious interest. And he could certainly get used to looking at the attractive woman at the other end of the couch. "I grew up in a small town where everybody had an opinion about everything and they didn't hesitate to offer it, whether you asked or not. The older I got, the more it bugged me. I mean, really pain-in-the-ass bugged me to the point where I'd do stuff just to get the rumors going. My old man was furious when he found out I was doing it to torment some of the busybodies. He said it was immature and disrespectful." Pete shook his head, recalled the days when he and his father had shouting matches that could be heard all the way down the street. "I was a jerk, but I never saw it that way. They sent me off to college and I made it through half of the second semester before I flunked out. You have no idea what it's like to come home to a place where everybody knows you flunked."

"I can't imagine."

The faint pink on her cheeks told him she'd probably never

jaywalked or gotten a speeding ticket. Well, he'd done both and a lot more back then. "It wasn't pretty, neither was the six o'clock start time in the cabinet factory where I worked because my father said I wasn't going to lie around like a cat all day and prowl all night."

She hid a smile. "I guess you'd call that tough love."

He raised a brow. "Yeah, something like that."

"Did you make amends with your father?"

Pete shrugged. "It's a work in progress. He's a no-nonsense kind of guy. Doesn't go in for deep thinking or fancy words. Don't kid yourself, though. He's one of the wisest men I ever met and it took me a lot of years to realize that." Actually, he hadn't figured that out until he was close to thirty, and when the business went belly up, he'd thought about his father's comments regarding true friends versus the ones who'll only show up as long as you're paying.

"What will you do when you finish here?"

Now that was the fifty-million-dollar question. He'd given it a lot of thought, but for a person who'd once believed he only had to blink to make money, he didn't have an answer. "I don't know. I've spent the last few months doing manual labor and I have to say, there's a certain reward that comes from creating and fixing things." He grinned, saluted her with his wine glass. "I've also mucked out my share of stalls and that would not be on the list of my life's ambition."

"So..." She tilted her head to one side, her long hair brushing her shoulders. He bet her hair was silky-soft, wondered if it smelled like the flowery scent in the bathroom. "You like creating and fixing things, you don't like mucking out stalls."

He nodded. "Right."

"Would you ever get back into real estate?"

That was a question he'd asked himself several times a day,

more so in the beginning, and not so much these past few weeks. Even if he were to consider it, there would have to be so many conditions, and the scenario would have to be perfect. "I really don't know. I was very good at it, but I wasn't a nice guy. I was a jerk who thought he couldn't lose." His voice dipped with remembering. "I made a lot of money, a sick amount, and I surrounded myself with people I thought were my friends, but they weren't. Friends tell you when you're screwing up and when you're full of yourself, but nobody ever did." He rubbed his jaw, met her gaze. "I don't want to be that guy anymore; that's what I do know."

"I'm glad."

Shit, had he just admitted he was a loser-asshole? Not exactly. He'd admitted he'd *been* one, as in past tense. That was different. Wasn't it? Pete clamped his mouth shut. He needed to cool it with the confessions for a while and get Elissa talking, but it was so damn easy to open up with her.

Why? Oh, right. Because they were *pretending* the outside world didn't exist. That's why. It wasn't like she had some special hold over him. He never let a woman close enough to get inside his head—not even Heather, and he'd thought of marrying her.

This whole "open up and share" had to do with the pretending stuff they'd decided on over dinner. He was cool with that. Very cool. As long as he understood what was happening and could control it. Pete blew out a sigh. "Your turn. What are you going to do when you leave here?"

"I'm a nurse. I worked in a hospital for a few years on a post-surgical floor, but what I enjoyed most was being a companion to a woman dying of cancer."

"Really? That sounds...depressing."

"It wasn't as depressing as it was sad. All the lost hopes and dreams." She sniffed and swiped at her eyes. "People our age have our own dreams and wishes, and we think we'll have years to see them fulfilled. But we don't really know, do we?" Another sniff. "Mrs. B was estranged from her family, so I became her family. I cooked for her, accompanied her on vacations and doctor visits. I even helped her plan her funeral, all according to her wishes. She was very precise, a true lady, and a friend." She cleared her throat, clasped her hands in her lap. "Yes, she was a friend to me, and all she asked was that I handle a few items of correspondence for her when she passed. That's all." Elissa sniffed again, dragged her gaze to his. "That's the least I can do for a friend, don't you think?"

Pete nodded. "Absolutely. It's the least you can do."

PETE SLEPT ON THE COUCH, wished it were a foot longer so his feet didn't hang off the edge, and he sure as hell wished it were more comfortable. But furniture was limited in this place and sharing a bed with Elissa—for sleeping— wasn't an option. Not that she'd invited him, because one look and three seconds with her told a guy she wasn't that type. Nope. This woman was the kind you brought home to meet your parents, married, moved with to the suburbs, and had a kid or two. He'd always been very good at spotting them—*and* avoiding them. Women like that weren't playing games; they were about relationships and commitments and the only reason he'd puked out his past to this one was because...because why? He dragged a hand over his face, blinked open his eyes. Oh, yeah, because they were miles away from anybody they knew, inside a cabin, and it was all pretend.

That made him feel better.

He sat up, padded into the kitchen, and started the coffee. There'd been a time, before Heather convinced him he needed a chef, that he'd enjoyed playing around in the kitchen, concocting dishes and taking a stab at growing his own herbs. She'd squashed that venture, insisting he didn't have time for such mindless endeavors. Why had he listened to her? Cooking and growing herbs relaxed him, gave him a sense of accomplishment. Pete thought of all the ways he'd been sidetracked in his life as he washed up, tossed on a fresh shirt, and fixed an omelet and rye toast.

"Elissa?" Pete knocked on the bedroom door, waited for a response, smiled when he heard a muffled groan. "Breakfast is ready." Another groan and an unintelligible response. "Hurry up or it'll be gone." That got her moving and sitting at the table by the time he poured her coffee.

"This is delicious," she said, forking a piece of mushroom and egg. "You should have called me." She glanced at him from a still-foggy haze of sleep. "I would have helped."

"No need. I like cooking, and it's been a while. Besides, we've got a full day ahead and I wanted you well rested. I posted a list on the refrigerator and if you're still game, we'll knock it out together."

She squinted at the fridge. "Sure."

"Do you know anything about painting?"

By late afternoon, he learned that not only did the woman know how to paint a room, she did a helluva job with trim work. No globs on the ceiling, no paint on the floor. Plus, she didn't flinch the way Heather used to when he played classic rock. Elissa liked it, sang to AC/DC and Bon Jovi. Damn, she even got him to belt out a few lines. That was no easy task.

Elissa had a lot going for her.

She didn't talk too much and when she did, the topics weren't filled with nonsense.

She didn't seem to need layers of makeup and hair products to start her day.

She listened. How was that for a novel approach to friendship?

She had a laugh that made him want to join in.

And when she looked at him, she really *looked*. Her lips were soft, her body curved in all the best places...

Crap. Pete pushed the man-in-hunting-mode thoughts aside and went back to the nonsexual assessments. Too late. His brain had wandered down the road of "how can you ignore the hot-blooded female in front of you" and once the thought was in his head, it spread to other parts of his body, the parts that had no business thinking about her. Damn it. Was he really going to ruin a good thing by being physically attracted to her? It wasn't as though she was drop-dead beautiful like Heather or any of the other women he'd dated. And she didn't have that I'm-going-to-have-you look that used to make him hard and planning for the party. Elissa had something more tantalizing, more compelling: fresh-faced honesty and words that didn't begin and end with sexual suggestions.

And that made her irresistible. He slid a gaze her way, landed on the roundness of her butt. Shit. He wanted her. So what? Wanting and having were not the same. Just because he wanted her did not mean he was going to have her.

Did it?

Well, did it?

The answer came the next evening, after dinner. They'd spent the day painting the dining room, and while Pete crawled on the roof to nail down loose shingles, Elissa picked up branches and twigs from the yard and tossed them into the trash bin for burning. Spring had made the area lush and green, the air crisp, filled with birds and the crackle of small animals in the woods. The fresh air and nature's surroundings brought him peace. When Pete glanced up from his hammering and spotted Elissa, face turned toward the sky, eyes closed, a perfect smile on her lips, that brought him peace, too.

They talked about what it would be like to live in the woods, debated whether will beat out strength—they both agreed it did—and how, on any given day, an ordinary person could accomplish an impossible task, given will and circumstances aligned.

There was so much to this woman that Pete didn't know, so much he wanted to uncover... She seemed equally curious to learn about him. Why? Was it because they'd shut out the world, or was there another reason, a deeper one involving fate and destiny?

"Fresh paint really does make a difference, doesn't it?"

"Huh?" He'd been thinking about fate and destiny, not the benefits of fresh paint. "Oh, right. If you want to knock a few years off something, paint it." That made her laugh and he guessed what she was thinking. "That doesn't include people."

She lifted her glass of wine, saluted him. "It was worth a try, wasn't it?"

"Trust me, you do not need to shave off any years." He studied the high cheekbones, the smooth skin, the full lips. "You'll be beautiful at seventy." Clearly, she wasn't used to compliments because her cheeks turned a pretty shade of pink, spread to her neck.

"My grandmother always said I was healthy-looking."

"You really don't like compliments, do you?" What woman didn't want to hear how beautiful she was? None that he'd known.

Elissa shook her head. "I'd rather you told me I was a decent person with a brilliant mind." She tucked a lock of dark hair behind her ear, cleared her throat. "We were raised to be practical. No room for big egos in our household."

"It's not like you've got your face stuck in a mirror. I'm beginning to wonder if you know how beautiful you are."

"Beautiful? Uh, no."

"You don't think you're eye-catchingly great-looking?"

"Of course not." She gulped the rest of her wine. "I've known people who are, like Zachary's other fiancée. I'm not one of those people, and I'm fine with that. It is what it is. If I were drop-dead beautiful then I'd have to worry about my hair and makeup being in place, and then I couldn't go in public unless I looked the part. No thank you. I'm fine with ordinary."

"Trust me, Elissa, you are not ordinary."

She actually laughed, as though she thought he were so far off base it wasn't funny. "Are you trying to seduce me?"

"What?" It was his turn to blush. "No, of course not."

"Oh."

She said it like she was disappointed. "Elissa? What's going on?"

She dragged her gaze to his. "If you were trying, I'd rather you didn't use a line on me."

"It wasn't a line." He paused, his voice thick with emotion. "And if we got together, it would not be a staged seduction."

"Good."

"It would be because..."

Her eyes sparkled. "Because..."

"We both wanted it?" he ventured.

Her lips parted. "Uh-huh."

Need fought with common sense; need won out. "So, do you..."

"Pete." She reached for him, kissed him with such passion, his world exploded. Hard. Heavy. Complete. Another kiss, this one deeper, more consuming.

He broke the kiss, cupped her chin with his fingers. "Are you sure?"

A dip of her head, followed by a breathy, "I don't want you to stop."

His conscience kicked in. Did she understand this wasn't going to be about more than lust and passion? "I'm no good at relationships."

"I'm not asking for a relationship."

Women like Elissa didn't outright ask, but the implication was there, especially when they said it wasn't. "I don't want to hurt you." He was dying to bury himself inside her right now, but she deserved more than just sex. Why couldn't she see that?

"I understand. You don't want a relationship." Her voice turned soft, swirled through him in a rush of heat. "I get it."

"I'm not sure you do." How many men had she known like him? A handful? Less than that?

"I'm a big girl. I know exactly what you are and aren't offering."

"Elissa."

"Stop talking." She reached for the top button of his shirt, rested a small hand on his belt buckle.

"I can't make promises."

"No promises." And then she smiled. "This is all pretend, right? We can do whatever we want and it's just the two of us."

But that wasn't quite true. He knew it as he eased the shirt over her head, unfastened her bra. Knew it when he cupped her breast, brought his lips to a nipple and sucked the sweetest, most tender flesh he'd ever tasted. And when they were both naked and their gazes locked seconds before he entered her in the purest free-fall of ecstasy he'd ever felt, the truth burned between them.

This was about so much more than sex.

This was real.

ELISSA AND PETE had spent the last twelve nights together, making love until they fell into an exhausted sleep, bodies tangled up in one another, breathing soft and even. Content. But the lovemaking wasn't confined to the bed or evenings. The need to be together in a physical way burned deep and bright between them. They'd made love after breakfast, against the kitchen counter, on a dining room chair, in the old tub. Outside, against the worn cabin siding. Goodness, they'd even made love in his truck after a return trip to town! She wanted him, all of him, and it seemed he felt the same way.

It had *never* been like this with Zachary or any other man. *Nobody was like Pete.* Nobody could make her tingle and burn or lose her inhibitions the way he did. And that scared her as much as it excited her.

She'd told him she knew they weren't long-term, that she understood he was no good at relationships and didn't expect one from him. When she'd said the words, she'd meant them, but that was before he touched her, before he filled her with want and need, before he showed her how good it could be between them. Not just the sex, but all of it. They'd worked side by side these past several days, fixing up the cabin, turning it into someone's home.

What would it be like if she and Pete lived here?

"Hey, sleepyhead. Plan to sleep all day?"

Pete stood in the doorway, long and lean, dressed in flannel and jeans. His gaze darted from the dip in the sheet that exposed a good portion of flesh, moved to her face. "You should have called me." She eased out of bed, stretched, enjoying the way his eyes followed her as she slipped into her panties and bra, pulled on a T-shirt. Elissa had never quite understood the sexual control some women exercised over men, maybe because she didn't think she was capable of it. She'd never felt overly sexual with Zachary, but with Pete, the push-pull of her sexuality wasn't intentional or contrived. It just *was*.

"Come here," he said, his voice rough, his expression unreadable. She moved toward him, placed her hands on his hips. He framed her face with his large hands, studied her. "The work's done here. We'll finish up today."

"I know."

"We can stay a while, or not, but whatever we decide to do, I need to be honest with you."

"Yes?" *Here it comes. He's going to tell me he's moving on...*

He cleared his voice twice. "I don't know about you, but for me, this pretending doesn't feel like pretending anymore."

Pete wasn't pretending; he cared about her, and he was going to admit it. Oh, but she wanted to hug him so tight and cry, but she didn't. Instead, she managed a serious "I know."

He pulled her to him, buried his lips in her hair. "I think we're going to have to talk about it."

"Uh-huh." Elissa closed her eyes, breathed in his scent, as the truth slipped out. She was falling in love with him. Could he find it in his heart to return that love?

The "talking" started later that afternoon, when Pete told her about Magdalena and the couples he'd observed. Of course, he didn't know she knew about Magdalena, and he certainly didn't know her connection to the heartache that almost happened there. How was she ever going to tell him about that? Or that she'd mailed the letter to Nate Desantro the day they drove into town? She'd have to tell him, but not yet.

"I've seen a lot of couples since I've been back in Magdalena. They're not crazy rich, not by most people's standards, at least not the ones I knew. But they're happy and they seem content. Some of them have been together for decades, others just a few years." They sat next to each other on the couch, his shoulder slung over hers, thighs touching, her head resting on his chest. "The ones our age are having kids, and they don't seem put out by the extra mouths to feed or annoyed they're giving up free time. Hell, they seem to enjoy it." He planted a kiss on the top of her head, murmured, "Maybe that's what real wealth is. You just have to find the right person to help you see that, and share it."

Elissa tightened her hold around his waist, whispered, "I think you're right."

"I'd like to have more money, but I'd rather have the right person beside me, step by step, through good times and not so good ones. My mother told me Nate Desantro had a rough road with his mother-in-law. The damn lady tried to break up his marriage with some fake seduction thing. Can you imagine that? What kind of parent does that to her own daughter?"

That's not what Mrs. Blacksworth had told her. She'd sworn Nate had been involved and he was the one to turn her daughter against her. "I'm sure there's more to the story."

"More? I doubt it unless you want to add psycho and witch to the mother-in-law's name."

Why would Mrs. Blacksworth lie to her? What was the point? Elissa wasn't a relative; she would not have judged. "I'm sorry," was all she could manage. She would have to tell Pete the truth, but not tonight. She'd tell him in the morning. And then she'd destroy the notebook.

"Look, I don't want to talk about her or whatever lies she told. All I know is my mother said she tried to ruin good people, and my mother's usually in the know about this stuff." He laughed, sifted a hand through her hair. "She's a little bit of a gossip. Drives my father crazy."

"I'll bet." When Pete heard her story, he'd understand, wouldn't he? He'd see that she'd believed a dying woman because she hadn't thought such a person capable of causing harm on her deathbed.

"Okay, now I'm really done with that woman." His voice gentled. "I want to talk about you and me." He paused, added. "Us."

Elissa sat up, hesitated. "Us?"

"Yeah. What I feel for you is real, not some pretend crap I made up to protect myself. I'd like to spend more time with you —" his eyes glittered, his voice dipped "—in the real world outside of the cabin. Will you come back to Magdalena with me? Meet my family?" A dull rose shot from his neck to his cheeks. "If you feel the same way, that is."

"I do...feel the same way." She stroked his cheek, kissed him. "I'll come with you. Anywhere you want to go."

"Let's stay here a few more days, and then we'll let the outside world bombard us, okay?"

"Uh-huh." She clung to him, wished she hadn't gotten involved with Mrs. Blacksworth's agenda. But there was no going back now; she'd done it and the sooner she told Pete the truth, the sooner they could move forward. They'd get past this. They cared about one another. People who cared about one another stuck together and forgave each other's missteps.

Didn't they?

6

Pete rose early the next morning, made the coffee, and started gathering their belongings. He sure was going to miss this place, but sooner or later, he and Elissa had to step into the real world and it might as well be in Magdalena. The people there would study Elissa with a keen eye, draw conclusions they may or may not put to sound, but in the end, they'd accept her. That's what small towns did. As long as she cared about him and didn't hurt him. You could move from a small town and stay away for fifteen years, but the second you walked back in, it was as if you'd never left, like you were still one of them—which you were.

He grabbed the bag of yarn and knitting needles he'd spotted on the couch the first day. The needles stuck out, but when Pete tried to push them into the bag, he noticed a notebook blocking the way. Pete eased it from the bag, studied it. Had Elissa pasted the red rose on the cover? Was this some sort of sketch book? He could picture her as an artist, sketching flowers and people. He smiled, flipped the notebook open, expecting to see a pencil sketch of a rose.

He did not expect to see Gloria Blacksworth's name

scrawled along the top border or the name *Magdalena* written in the margins. *What the hell?* Pete sank onto the couch and began to read...

Forty minutes later, he closed the notebook, stared at the cover with the pasted rose. How could Elissa be capable of such cold-hearted cruelty? What did it mean? Had she copied pages from Gloria Blacksworth's notebook and created her own?

Did she plan to continue the torment once she sent the final letter?

Was she blackmailing people?

Who could tell? He sure as hell couldn't, not after reading the contents and the side notes she'd written. Damn her for pretending to be kind and caring, a human being with a conscience...

"Pete?"

The sweetness of her voice swept over him, almost made him wish he hadn't opened the notebook and learned the harsh truth about her. But what was the point of prolonging what would turn out to be a bad ending? Had he really thought he might have a future with the woman? A stranger, no less, whose sob story wasn't half as sickening as the drama inside the notebook. Elissa could have ended it all when the Blacksworth woman died, but she didn't. Hell no, she carried on the legacy, as a favor to a *friend*.

"Pete?"

She stood in the kitchen doorway, wearing his flannel shirt, long legs bare, a hint of a smile on her lips. Fresh-faced, innocent, tempting. A seductress bent on destruction. He slid the notebook across the table. "Look what I found. A play-by-play book on how to destroy lives."

The second she realized what it was, she lunged toward the table and snatched up the notebook. "You...you read this?"

He shrugged. "Twice."

"I planned to tell you today." The words spilled out in a rush of panic. "I didn't know Mrs. Blacksworth was lying. I believed what she told me. I thought I was honoring a dead woman's request by mailing the letters."

That pissed him off. He pushed back the chair, stood. "You didn't know she was lying? You thought these letters were normal? They could destroy lives!" Pete moved toward her, stopped when he was an arm's length away. "This Blacksworth woman is the friend you were talking about, isn't she? She sounds sick in the head, a pariah, a mental cancer that eats at you."

She shook her head, inched her gaze back to his. "I didn't know. I don't think she was like that in the beginning."

"Of course, she was like that." How could he have thought this woman was special? She was worse than Heather; at least his old girlfriend had never tried to be anything other than the society girl she was. But Elissa? Hell, she'd acted like goodness was her middle name.

"You didn't know her. She was all alone...and dying," she stammered, her eyes bright. "I think she lost her way."

Let the damn tears come. He would not be taken in by them or the crushed look on her beautiful face. "Your definition of friendship is twisted."

"I believed her." Her voice split open with sadness. "All she wanted was for me to mail the letters. How could I say no? She told me it was her duty to see them delivered, that fate would help the innocents involved."

Was she serious? "That is such bullshit. How could you believe that crap? Look what she wrote about the MacGregors. Would a decent person expose a pregnancy? And Nate Desantro. Were you involved in that mess?" When she didn't answer, anger fueled his next words. "Tell me, damn it."

The tears spilled down her cheeks, to her chin, her neck,

landed on the flannel shirt. "I didn't want to hurt anyone." Her lips quivered, her shoulders shook. "I only wanted to honor my word."

"Yeah, you did that, and who knows what damage you caused in the process. And what about Jack Finnegan?" He'd saved this one for last. According to her side notes, she hadn't mailed the letter yet. Taking money didn't sound like his father, but if he had done it, then the old man had a reason, a good one, and it shouldn't be brought into the open. Period. "Answer me."

She shook her head, sniffed. "I'm sorry. I never meant to hurt anyone. I know you care about the people in this town..."

Those last words shot through him. "Sure, you do. Last night, when I told you about Magdalena and Nate, you never said a word. Did you think I wouldn't care that you'd tried to torch the place where I grew up? Or did you think I'd never find out?"

"No." More tears. "I didn't know how to tell you about the Desantros because then you'd ask how..."

"Why not just lie? That's what you've been doing all along, right?" The damn pain in his gut burned, shot through the rest of his body.

"That's not true. I planned to tell you about the notebook today."

"Ah, now isn't that convenient?" Those hazel eyes poured tears, begged him to understand. Oh, he understood, he understood what it felt like to get played. Pete buried the hurt and said, "You're gonna destroy this book. Right now, before any more harm comes to anyone."

"I planned to burn it," she said in a small voice.

"Sure you did. Tell me, was it a sudden burst of conscience that brought you to that decision?"

"No. I mailed the last letter the other day when we went to town."

"Last letter?" There was only one letter that hadn't been sent yet. He clenched his fists, waited for her response.

"The one about Jack Finnegan. I mailed it to Nate Desantro."

"Damn you!" Pete grabbed the notebook and the pack of matches in the cupboard above the sink. "Get dressed." He began tearing pages from the book as he made his way outside. When he reached the backyard, he dumped the book and the random pages in the trash bin, lit a match, and tossed it inside. "Burn, you bastard, burn." Flames captured the pages, destroyed the words that could harm others. He glanced up, spotted Elissa staring at him from the kitchen window. How could he have been such a fool? She'd torched his heart, but only because he'd given her the opportunity *and* the ammunition to do it.

Pete blew out a sigh of disgust, looked away, and pulled out his cell phone. If he were lucky, he'd intercept the letter before it reached Nate and brought a shit storm to the Finnegans. He punched in his father's number, waited.

"Hello?"

"Dad? Listen, there's a letter coming to Nate from one of Gloria Blacksworth's friends." He paused, drew in a deep breath. "It's about some money that went missing several years back." The hitched breath on the other end of the line told him his father knew exactly what he was talking about. "You need to contact Nate and tell him not to open the letter."

"Son, I'm sorry—"

"You gotta get that letter, Dad. Nate can't read it."

"I never wanted any of you kids to find out. It's the worst decision I ever had to make in my life." He paused, his voice cracking. "Steal from a friend or let one of our family be disgraced."

"What are you talking about? Who would've been disgraced?" Was it one of Pete's siblings? If it happened twenty-some years ago, it had to be an older kid. Which one? And what kind of trouble that involved three thousand dollars?

"I can't say. It's private and no matter all the years that've passed, this person wouldn't survive the telling." A deep sigh. "I'm just real sorry you had to learn that your old man isn't as upstanding as he pretends to be."

Pete pictured his father sitting in his favorite rocker, shoulders slumped, rough hands clasped together, his blue eyes a mix of pain and sadness. He cleared his throat, pushed out the words he'd known for years but had never spoken. "You're the best person I know, Dad, and I'm proud you're my father. I'm the one who's sorry for acting like a shit all these years, taking the easy way out while you made tough choices for us. I'm not going to let this damn letter take you down or ruin your relationship with Nate. I'm going to fix this."

"How, son? How can you fix a wrong you didn't create? If anybody's going to make amends, it's got to be me. But I sure do appreciate the effort. Means a lot." Long pause. "How'd you find out about the letter, son?"

Now there was the big question. Pete fumbled for an answer and settled on, "A woman."

His father whistled through the line. "Damn, isn't that always the way?"

"Sure looks like it."

"I'll see you when you finish up there, and don't worry about me. This conversation with Nate has been a long time coming, and I'd just as soon be done with it than carry it on my back another twenty-some years. And, son?"

"Yes?"

"Don't be too hard on the woman." *Click.*

Pete stared into the trash bin as the remnants of the notebook turned into charred bits of memories, their threat nothing more than black bits of ash. *Don't be too hard on the woman.* Since when had his father softened on what constituted right and wrong? Back in the day, Jack Finnegan believed in black and white choices, no gray allowed. Still, this wasn't about his father's rules or beliefs. This was about Pete and what he'd thought Elissa stood for, who he believed she was, and worse, how incredibly wrong he'd been about both. Again.

"Pete?"

Elissa stood a few feet away, dressed in jeans and a sweatshirt, her ski vest unzipped, hands gloveless. No hat. Hadn't she told him she never went outside without layers of cold-weather gear? Yeah, she had, but maybe she'd even been lying about something as inconsequential as dressing for the weather. Who knew? Who cared? He shoved his hands in his back pockets, welcoming the chilly air that whipped through his open jacket. He sure didn't care. Not. One. Bit. "What do you want?"

She inched closer, peered in the trash bin. "I'm glad you burned the notebook."

How to respond to that? "I only wish I'd found it before you sent the last letter."

"You know this Jack Finnegan, don't you?"

"I know him." He held her gaze and let the truth spill out. "He's my father."

"Your...father?"

The shock on her face gave him a small amount of satisfaction. So, she really hadn't known who he was. Well, now she did. "He's the man I told you about, remember? The one who gave me a hard time and pretty much kicked my lazy butt out of town? He's also the best person I know, and your allegiance to that Blacksworth woman is going to hurt him. I don't know how

Nate Desantro's going to take it, but it wasn't your secret to tell." Pete swore under his breath. "I am so damn tired of this conversation."

"I'm so sorry."

"You're sorry? Save the 'sorry's' and the tears. It's too late for them. It only mattered when you could have told me the truth and didn't." Logic told him to stop here and let it go, but logic had vanished the second he met this woman. "Last night I told you I was from Magdalena, and I told you about the Desantros. You had to have figured I had a connection to them if I was fixing their cabin. And you never said a damn word." He planted his hands on his hips, glared at her. "Nothing. You let me think you were some wounded angel dropped from the sky, unlike any I'd ever met before, and I was going to be the one to save you." The laugh that spilled from him was cold, harsh, brittle. "But you're no angel. You're a woman without a conscience."

"No." She shook her head. "Don't say that."

"You played me, didn't you? From the very beginning."

The tears started up again, clogged her speech. "That's not true. I cared about you. I care about you," she corrected.

"Sure you do." Pete rubbed his jaw, sighed. "You care so much you forgot to tell me you were going to destroy people *I* care about, including my father."

"I didn't know he was your father, and I didn't know you were from Magdalena...not at first." Her words spilled over him, begged him to understand.

"You had a good idea I wasn't just a stranger to the Desantros, though, didn't you?"

"The truth? I was more interested in getting to know *you* and the more I learned, the more I wanted to mean something to you."

Pete tried to spot the lies in those words. Damn, but he

couldn't see them. That didn't mean they weren't there. He had to protect himself, even if it meant he'd be the one telling the lies. "You wanted to mean something to me, huh?" Those hazel eyes glistened with fresh tears as she nodded. He opened his mouth, let the lies spill. It was the only way to save himself from a world of misery. "We were pretending, remember? None of what happened in the cabin was real. We needed a break and a little physical companionship, and that's exactly what we got." He clenched and unclenched his fist, forced out the rest while he still had the guts to do it. "I don't know about you, but the touchy-feely stuff I unloaded on you? That was for your benefit because women like a man who's got feelings."

"You...you made it all up? You're not broke, your girlfriend didn't dump you...you didn't lose your house and cars..."

It hurt to smile, but he made those damn lips freeze in place. How else could he convince her to believe his lies? This was about self-preservation and survival—his. Pete shrugged as if the answers didn't matter. She stared at him so long he thought any second she'd lunge at him, go for his eyes, his face, maybe his groin. But she didn't. Elissa, whose last name he didn't know, swiped her cheeks one last time, straightened her shoulders, turned, and walked toward the house, taking any hope of a second chance and happiness with her.

WHEN NATE GOT the phone call from Jack saying he needed to see him right away, he thought it had to do with the old guy's health. Or his wife's. Dolly Finnegan battled extra pounds and rising blood sugar, but she refused to give up the chocolate eclairs from the bakery. Or the bacon. Jack tried to help, but he had no patience for those who refused to do what they needed to; he usually ended up in a shouting match with Dolly, which elevated *his* blood pressure and gave him a headache.

The Finnegans had been married a lot of years, raised five children, and made a vow early on never to go to bed mad. According to Dolly, they'd kept that vow, but when Jack called today, he'd sounded on edge and jittery, like he was about to explode.

Nate hoped it wasn't his health or Dolly's. Or something to do with Pete.

Pete Finnegan was a wild card. They'd all heard about the money he'd made in real estate, the houses, the cars, the travel. The women. And then they'd heard he'd lost it all. Some said it was gambling. Others said a woman took it. Still others said it was bad luck and a worse market. Who could tell?

Nate didn't care. He didn't even care if the guy once owned suits that cost more than some of Nate's tools. Not his business. Not anybody's business. He scratched his jaw, sighed. Tell that to the residents of Magdalena. They'd be sniffing around and making up tales that belonged on television or in the tabloids. Pete should be back in town in a few days, and then the cabin could go up for sale, and Christine could put one more sad memory behind her.

They'd had a few "lively" discussions about her father's letters, and Christine had agreed that his mother and Lily should receive theirs. Harry's letter was the problem. How could Christine think any good could come from letting the guy read it? Harry was soft and kind, good-natured and a friend to kids and animals. It would destroy him, and Nate was not going to watch that happen. One way or another, that letter was getting burned or shredded.

Harry would never know it existed. Nate just needed a little more time to persuade his wife that this was the right decision. He tossed the pencil on his desk, rubbed his eyes, yawned. The baby had been up most of the night with an earache and that meant no sleep for anybody. The joys of family life. Another yawn. He wouldn't trade it for anything...

"Am I disturbing your nap?"

Nate looked up, squinted at his old friend. "Hey, Jack. Come on in." Jack Finnegan removed his ball cap, closed the office door, and sat in one of the chairs opposite Nate's desk. His weather-beaten face looked pale beneath the perpetual tan, his cheeks crisscrossed with lines of worry. Damn, but Nate bet this had to do with Dolly. "What's going on?"

Jack shook his head, his blue eyes settling on Nate. "I'm ashamed of what I'm about to tell you, Nate. Ashamed it happened in the first place, but more ashamed I didn't own up to it a long time ago." There was a pause, followed by two throat clearings, and then silence.

Nate waited a few more seconds before he spoke. "You're going to have to help me out here because I don't know what you're talking about."

Jack toyed with the ball cap in his hands, dragged his gaze to Nate's. "There's no fancy way to say it, except to say it and tell you I'm real sorry." One more throat clearing. "I take it you didn't get a letter from somebody today that had to do with your dead mother-in-law?"

That got his attention. Nate leaned forward, hands flat on the top of the desk. "No, I didn't get any letter. Why? Who's she trying to blackmail now?" How the hell could a dead woman still be trying to destroy families? And what did Jack have to do with it?

"She's after me this time." He paused, bit his lower lip. "That's not true. She's still after you, but she's going to use me to do it. If you didn't get the letter yet, I hear it's on its way."

"And how do you know this?"

"Sources. Pete called to warn me. How he found out about

this whole mess is a mystery, but I think there's a woman involved somewhere along the way. And I think she's the one that's got something to do with the letter. That's all I know."

Nate rubbed his jaw, considered what Jack had just told him. How many people knew about Gloria Blacksworth's notebook? Of those who knew, how many were women? The only one he could think of was the caregiver Gloria hired before she died. A nursing student, completely naïve to her employer's manipulative ways. "I might know who that is."

"Then you know more than me. Pete never was much of a talker when it came to his female companions. Don't guess he's gotten much better with age, but he told me enough to warn me."

"Warn you the letter's coming?"

"Yup. It's coming and it's meant to cause a world of problems between us." Jack shook his head, heaved a big sigh. "I sure wish I didn't have to give this speech, but I should have done it twenty-nine years ago."

"Twenty-nine years? What the hell are you talking about?" Did this have to do with Nate's father? Had Nick Desantro been involved with some underhanded dealings in the business and Jack found out once the old man died? Of course, Jack would keep it from Nate, try to shoulder the knowledge to protect other people. That's the kind of man Jack Finnegan was: trustworthy, honorable. A good friend.

"I took three thousand dollars from ND Manufacturing."

"Come again?" Had he just said he took money from the company?

The older man's shoulders slumped like that money was weighing him down and when he spoke, his voice turned brittle and cracked. "I had a family predicament and I needed the money. With five mouths to feed, me and Dolly struggled to keep the kids in coats and sneakers. There was no way I could come up with that kind of cash." He pinched the bridge of his nose, cleared his throat. "But I couldn't stand by and watch a good person destroyed because of ignorance and trusting the wrong person. I paid it all back, with interest. It took me three years to do it, and Dolly never knew." His blue gaze narrowed. "And she's never gonna know."

Nate studied the man who'd served as a better role model than his own father. All these years together and he'd never guessed there was a giant lie between them. "What kind of problem could make you take money?" He paused, finished with the most painful part, "From me?" Jack Finnegan was the kind of guy who *returned* money when a cashier messed up in his favor. Stealing—and that's what taking three thousand dollars from ND Manufacturing was—did not fit Jack Finnegan's personality or history. It wasn't who the man was... and yet he'd done it. What did that say about what a person would do in a desperate situation?

There was only one question left to ask.

"What was so damn urgent that you had to steal from the company?"

Jack shook his head, hands clutching the ball cap he wore every day so hard the cap was half its size. "I can't say, Nate. I'm sorry. It would..." He cleared his throat, his eyes bright. "It would destroy the person in question and I can't do that. I kept my mouth shut all these years, didn't even tell Dolly and there's nothing she doesn't know about me." The blueness in those eyes turned bluer. "But not this."

"You're putting me in a terrible position. You just told me you stole from the company, and you won't even give me details to defend your actions? What am I supposed to do with that, Jack? Huh? Am I supposed to pretend this never happened? Damn it, I wish you'd never told me." There weren't more than a handful of people Nate trusted and Jack was one of them. Or had been. Could he still trust the man? His gut told him he could, but the hurt in him wondered.

The man who'd helped him through more than one bad time stood, cleared his throat. "Like I said, I should have told you years ago, but I couldn't stand the thought of seeing you look at me like you're doing now. Disgusted. Disappointed." He shrugged, clutched that damn cap harder. "But I was not gonna let that letter arrive and take you by surprise. I couldn't do that."

"Appreciate it." Nate eased back in his chair, waited for Jack to continue.

"I expect you're gonna do what you gotta do, and I'm fine by that. All I ask is that you tell the guys I left to spend more time fishing." He worked up an almost smile. "They'll believe that."

"What do you mean? You're quitting?"

The almost smile inched up. "I always thought I'd end up like your old man, taking my last breath on the shop floor. I love this place, Nate. Had a lot of good times here; some bad ones, too, but I wouldn't trade them for anything. But I think I'll leave now, save you having to give me the ax." He plunked the ND Manufacturing ball cap on his head, nodded. "If you want, I'll hang around until you get a new foreman in place. There's some good men on the floor that would do you proud." Jack extended a hand across the desk, tears rimming his eyes. "It's been a real pleasure, Nate. A real pleasure. I couldn't be prouder of you than if you were one of my own."

Nate ignored the other man's extended hand, pushed back his chair and made his way to the other side of the desk. "Can't you tell me anything about why you did what you did?"

Jack shook his head. "It's not about me or saving my hide. It's about protecting a person from a past that won't let go. I can't do it. I'm sorry."

The man left him with two choices. Nate could accept the

resignation and maybe he'd eventually convince himself that Jack Finnegan wasn't as honest or trustworthy as he'd once thought. Or, he could accept the man's refusal to divulge the reason for taking the money and move on. Deep down, he knew Jack wasn't a thief, knew he could be trusted, and that he cared about Nate. You had to respect a man who would give up the job he loved and risk the respect of a friend to protect someone in need. "So, my choice is to let this incident go or let you go?"

Jack eased his outstretched hand to his side "Don't see it as much of a choice. You've always been about honor and doing right."

"Yeah, I have been, haven't I?" He narrowed his gaze on his friend. "And I'm going to trust my gut and stick with that."

"I expected as much."

This time, it was Nate who held out his hand. "I guess I'll never understand what you did, but I understand why you did it. You helped a family member in trouble. That's doing the right thing. *That's* showing honor." He gripped Jack's hand with both of his. "I need you here, being my eyes and ears, keeping me on track. You know me almost as well as Christine."

The old man shrugged, worked up a smile. "Don't think I like the sound of that."

Nate grinned. "Take the compliment and shut up, okay?"

Jack's smile faded, his voice cracked. "You sure about this? I'm giving you a way out. No hard feelings."

If his wife had taught him one thing, it was that every relationship suffered bumps and bruises along the way. That's what made them stronger, gave them the calluses to withstand the rocky paths that cropped up now and again. Jack Finnegan was worth a callus or two. "I'm sure. When the letter arrives, I'll burn it, and we'll leave what happened twenty-nine years ago where it belongs—in the past."

7

Elissa would always wonder when she realized Mrs. Blacksworth wasn't the wounded soul she'd once thought she was, or how the woman had manipulated her to carry out deeds that were more about vengeance than exposing wrongdoing and helping victims.

Pete Finnegan was gone. He'd packed up the truck, done a final walk-through of the cabin, made sure his punch list was complete, and then he'd given her a brief nod and left. No words, no lingering gazes.

Nothing.

This loss was more painful than finding out about Zachary. She'd shown Pete who she really was, and she'd believed he'd done the same. Sure, they'd called it pretending, but that wasn't anything more than a safe way to let the other person see the scars and the hurts. It was a way to gain acceptance without judgment, and maybe even love. She would not believe their time together meant nothing to him, and she refused to accept that he'd lied to her about his life in California.

But how would she ever know? She'd ruined their chance. What might have happened if she'd told him she knew Nate and Christine Desantro, knew about Magdalena, and had a part in causing pain to some of the residents? Would she have realized her employer's motives sooner? Would Pete have judged her, and if he had, would he have forgiven her?

Maybe.

Or maybe not.

She'd lived her whole life according to right and wrong, well-crafted plans and life timelines, and yet, she'd never been unhappier. The only moments of true, pure happiness had been the time spent in the cabin with Pete.

And she'd ruined it. All of it. Her chest ached with the loss she'd brought on with her naïveté. She made her way to the bedroom, lay on Pete's pillow, inhaled his scent. If she closed her eyes, she could almost pretend he was in the kitchen, making breakfast as he'd done these past several days. The smell of coffee would reach her any second, then the aroma of cinnamon and apples as he heated them for her oatmeal and topped it with walnuts. Soon, he'd carry a tray into the bedroom, humming under his breath. And then he'd kiss her temple...whisper in her ear...

Elissa blinked her eyes open, swiped at her cheeks.

She could pretend all she wanted because Pete was gone. Gone from the cabin, gone from her life. But the memory of him? That would never disappear. Life would be different now. No more five-year plans or timelines, no more following someone else's blueprint or definition of happiness.

If the time in the cabin had taught her one lesson, it was that life could and should be lived on her own terms, no matter the outcome. Tomorrow, she'd close up the place and head back to Chicago. Maybe she'd stop along the way, look for a few small towns to spend the night. What was the rush? Her parents didn't expect her for another week and she wasn't due back at work for another ten days—just in time to hand in her resignation. People would think she was crazy to quit a nursing job that paid so well, but it wasn't about the money. Mrs. Blacksworth had gifted her a generous sum, but even if she hadn't, Elissa would still leave. Maybe it was the hospital setting she didn't like...or maybe it was Chicago...

She didn't know, not yet, but she'd explore the possibilities until she found a place and a job that brought her joy.

∼

"Dad says he loves me more than three scoops of cherry chip ice cream." *Giggle giggle.* "That's his very favorite." Lily's eyes sparkled as she read the lines from the letter her father had written her. "He loves me more than snow angels on a starry night." Her voice drifted. "He's an angel now," she whispered, glancing at Christine, who sat next to her. "A real one, not just a snow one. And he can see everything we're doing." She pointed toward the ceiling, nodded. "He watches over all of us."

Christine nodded, whispered back, "Yes, he does."

"Anna and Joy, too, even though he never met them when he was on earth."

"Yes" Christine said, her voice cracking, "them, too."

Nate watched his sister discuss angels as though she believed everyone knew they existed and it was no big deal to carry on conversations with them. Only Lily. He and Christine delivered the letters to his mother and Lily this afternoon while Lucy Benito babysat the girls. They'd agreed the less distractions, the better. When Christine handed his mother her letter, she'd clutched it to her chest, let out a whimper, and disappeared into the bedroom.

Yeah, he got how she'd want to be alone.

"Dad loves me more than ten flannel shirts!" Lily looked at

Nate, brows pulled together. "Do you love Christine more than ten flannel shirts?"

That sounded like a Lily question. He grinned and slid a glance at his wife. "Ten? That's a lot." He rubbed his jaw, pretended to consider his answer.

"Come on, Nate." Lily leaned toward him. "Tell her."

"Well..." His voice dipped as he held Christine's gaze. "Actually, I love Christine more than *five hundred* flannel shirts."

"Yay!" Lily clapped her hands, laughed. "I knew it."

"I figured you did." He grinned at his sister.

She gave him the thumbs-up and went back to the letter. He spotted the second her mood changed. Her mouth pulled into a frown, her small shoulders sagged. When she looked up, there were tears in her eyes. "Dad says he can't wait to be here for my first horse ride." *Sniff, sniff.* "He didn't get to come because he died." *Sniff, sniff.* "I miss him so much."

Christine put an arm around Lily, pulled her close. "I know, sweetheart. I know."

Nate didn't miss the raspy voice or the tears in his wife's eyes. Damn, but he hated to see a woman in tears, especially his wife and sister. He guessed his mother might be shedding a few of her own since she'd been in the bedroom the past forty minutes. "Hey, this letter was supposed to make you happy, not turn you into a sad sack."

"I know." She sneaked a peek at him, swiped her eyes from beneath her glasses.

Since Lily believed in angels, then he'd give her a good thought to hold onto. "You know your dad was watching you ride, don't you? I mean, you couldn't see him because he was high up in the sky, but he saw you." The sniffing stopped and she grew very still. "Who do you think protected you from getting more than a broken leg when you jumped the fence? You don't think that was luck, do you?"

"It was Dad, wasn't it?" she asked, her voice filled with wonder.

He shrugged. "Who can say? You're the one who tells us about angels and how your dad's one of them. Doesn't it make sense that he'd keep an eye on you and Christine?"

Lily's head bobbed up and down. "Uh-huh."

He smiled at her, held out his arms. "Come here, kiddo. Give me a hug."

She sprang off the couch and rushed toward him, flinging her arms around his neck. "I love you, Nate."

He stroked her hair, whispered, "I love you too, kiddo. More than five hundred flannel shirts."

The tears stopped after that, replaced with laughter and stories about Anna and Joy's latest antics. Lily loved being an aunt and told them she wouldn't mind another niece or nephew. She said it with such conviction that Nate and Christine couldn't find the words to tell her couples didn't have more children because someone wanted to be an aunt. But then Lily shrugged and her next words made Nate wonder if she'd been playing them all along.

"It doesn't have to be a two-legged niece or nephew." Her lips pulled into a big smile and she said, "A four-legged one is fine, too. What do you think about that?"

Fortunately, they didn't have to answer because Miriam appeared in the living room doorway, nose red, eyes puffy. She made her way to Nate and Christine, hugged first one and then the other. "Thank you. Thank you very much."

And then she turned and disappeared back into her bedroom.

Harry didn't find out about the letters until late the next afternoon. He knocked on Nate and Christine's front door with a bottle of bourbon and six sticky buns, fresh baked and iced this morning.

"Greta's a keeper," he said, easing one of the sticky buns from the container and handing it to Christine. "She knows I can't resist these things; makes them for me and the kids once a month."

Nate pointed to the bourbon. "Does she know you can't resist *that* either?"

Harry laughed. "Those days are gone. I'll have a drink or two, but I'm not swimming in the stuff like I used to..." He let out another laugh. "I got too damn much to do. Kids and a wife who depend on me. I can't afford to get bleary and out of focus." Harry shook his head, lowered his voice. "Greta would clobber me if I stepped out of line, and besides, I'm not gonna disappoint her."

"Spoken like a husband who knows how to keep peace in the household." Nate grinned, set a glass of water in front of him. "So, what's going on?"

"Is everything okay, Uncle Harry?" This from Christine. "Your phone call worried me."

His blue gaze slid from his niece to Nate. "Nah. Nothing serious." He shrugged, sipped his water. "I heard you found a few things at the cabin." He paused, rubbed his jaw. "Letters from Charlie?"

Damn, how had he found out about the letters? "Who's the little bird that's been chirping?"

He shrugged. "Who else? Lily."

Of course, it would be Lily. She was so excited about her letter, she'd decided to memorize every word of it, and his mother told him she'd slept with it under her pillow last night. "How did I not see this coming?"

Christine raised a brow. "Did you see the play for the four-legged family member coming yesterday? She's a sharp one, and very crafty."

"Huh?" Harry placed both elbows on the counter, clasped his hands together. "What did Lily do now?"

"She tried to talk us into a pet by saying she wanted to be an aunt again." Christine shook her head. "It was very clever. And when she saw our shocked expressions, she backtracked and said four-legged additions to the family counted, too."

Harry threw back his head and roared. "Ah, that's my Lily Girl. I'll lay money you'll have a pup by summer."

"Don't count on it," Christine said, "A puppy's like another baby and we've got our hands full."

Nate considered his wife's response, slid in an alternative. "We could always rescue a dog that's a few years old."

"Rescue? A few years old?" She looked from Nate to Harry. "I haven't had a dog since I was a child."

Her uncle raised a brow. "So? Every kid should have a dog. Teaches them responsibility, right?" He paused, his face shifting to pink. "Greta and I are thinking about getting one for our gang. I'm the one who wants one, but I'm going to blame it on the kids." More pink, swirling to his ears. "What do you think about a Great Dane? I like the name Felix."

Christine shook her head. "I think no."

Nate crossed his arms over his chest, pretended to study Harry, and said, "You seem more like a Chihuahua kind of guy."

"Screw you." Harry laughed. "Greta made me promise to talk to one of those people who match the dog with the owner and the lifestyle. You know, don't get a dog that needs three hours of exercise if you live on the couch. Don't pick one because you think he has pretty eyes, that kind of crap." He tore off a section of sticky bun, popped it in his mouth and chewed. "Who would have thought people got paid to do stuff like that? Is that even a real job?"

Nate shrugged. "Dunno. Did you come here to talk about dogs? I've got a list of honey-do things to get done and your niece isn't going to be happy if I don't at least get them started." He knew the dog conversation was Harry's way of easing into the real reason he'd stopped by—the letters. But if the man didn't ask his questions soon, it would be dinnertime and he'd still be yakking about dogs and trainers.

"Greta wanted me to deliver the sticky buns, and I did have a question or two about dogs, but that's not why I'm here." The blueness in his eyes shifted to silver. "Were there any more letters?"

Nate darted a glance at his wife. She'd gone pale. He waited for her to respond, and when she didn't, he jumped in. "Charlie wrote one to Christine, one to me." Long pause. "And one to Gloria."

"Oh." His voice turned rough. "Huh. Guess I didn't rate."

There was no missing the hurt in his voice, but hurt was a helluva lot better than despair, and that's right where Harry would be if he read the letter intended for him. "Maybe he ran out of time," Nate said. *Or maybe he didn't...maybe the letter was tucked in the top desk drawer fifty feet away.*

"Yeah." Harry shrugged. "Maybe."

"Uncle Harry." Christine clasped his hand, leaned forward, eyes bright.

Here it comes. She's going to tell him.

"Dad loved you. You know that."

She's going to blow his world apart. She's going to tell him about the letter.

"I loved him, too, Chrissie," Harry said, his voice hoarse. "So, no letter, huh?"

"No," she whispered, a tear spilling down her cheek. "No letter."

∼

THE LAST TIME Pete saw his Aunt Edith he'd been twenty years old. She'd hugged him tight and slipped an envelope in his pocket containing two hundred dollars and a prayer card of St. Christopher, the patron saint of travelers. She said the money and the prayer card seemed fitting as he was about to embark on a cross-country journey in a vehicle of questionable reliability and might require money and prayers to reach his destination. She'd been right. The water hose burst outside of Omaha, and the cash, along with St. Christopher, guided him to California.

Today, he sat in her front parlor as he had fifteen years ago, and like then, she hugged him and tried to shove money in his pocket. This time, the hug wasn't as strong and the envelope contained deeds to several acres in and around Magdalena.

"Aunt Edith, I'm not accepting this." Pete laid the envelope on the coffee table and turned to her. "I appreciate the offer, but I don't need help. Besides, you might need these one day." The deeds contained tracts of land that covered sixteen acres. Everybody knew the area was rich in timber, and if you partitioned off the land, you'd have quite a few lots, Hell, you could plan a small development if you wanted.

But that would destroy the feel of the community. Magdalena's quaintness would be lost to new construction, overpopulation, and traffic. Way too much traffic. Pete liked progress, but some places should be protected from the hustle-bustle of overbuilding, and Magdalena was one of them. At twenty, he'd been anxious to get out of the small town where everyone knew everyone else's business, but at thirty-five, he'd developed an appreciation for quiet and having a few friends who knew you back when, as opposed to a roomful who didn't know you at all.

"Peter, I've been waiting for the day you'd come back here." Her thin lips pulled into a frown. "I'd hoped you'd bring a wife and a baby or two." She let out a long sigh that sounded an awful lot like sadness mixed with regret. "But there's still time. You do want a wife and children, don't you?"

Visions of a fresh-faced woman with dark hair and hazel eyes squeezed his chest. He pushed them away, picked up one of the store-bought vanilla cookies his aunt had set out. "If the opportunity presents itself, I'd be open to it." *And if the woman in question wasn't keeping a notebook filled with secrets and destruction...*

"You'd be *open* to it?" She shook her head, sniffed. "What does that mean? Love isn't a negotiation, my boy; it's magical and wondrous and has great powers. You weren't here when Daniel and Tess Casherdon were tested by fate. Twice. Oh, but they struggled; first torn apart by tragedy, and later, by another woman." She *tsk-tsked* as though she were commenting on a movie and not real people's lives. "I never gave up on them, no, I did not, even when it looked like there was no hope for them." She took a sip of tea, said in a voice as soft as cotton balls, "Love prevails. Always." Her gaze slipped over him, settled on his face. "You've had a bit of heartache, haven't you, Peter?"

He coughed, cleared his throat. "No. Of course not." Why would she say that? Was it because he was thirty-five and hadn't brought home a wife and child?

More *tsk-tsking*, this time aimed at him and his life. "I recognize heartbreak when I see it and you're a man suffering from it." She dabbed her eyes with her napkin and clasped his hand. "I want to help you. Tell me about her."

"I'm sorry, Aunt Edith, but there isn't anyone." He worked up a smile. "Just me and my sorry self."

"If that's true, then it's only because you haven't admitted it to yourself yet. I'm a patient woman, Peter. When you admit you're in love, you just remember your Aunt Edith was the first to know." She patted his hand and nodded. "In the meantime, let's talk about how to go about transferring the deeds."

8

TWO MONTHS LATER

The sun beat on Pete's head, made him wish he'd borrowed one of his father's ball caps. If the local weatherman hadn't missed his target, it was going to be another hot one. Heat was relative, and it hadn't bothered him when he lived in California. But he hadn't *lived* in the heat; he'd lived in the air-conditioning. Who couldn't tolerate a cool room with a programmable thermostat? Same with his car—punch a few buttons and the heat evaporated within minutes, leaving the interior crisp and fresh.

But Pete wasn't in California and he sure as hell wasn't in air-conditioning. Nope. He was walking the land his Aunt Edith had gifted him, trying to decide which plots to give his siblings. After a bit of deliberation and persuasion, his aunt agreed it might cause a family feud if Pete kept the land all to himself, *but* he was to keep the majority. Period. It wasn't open for discussion or debate. When Pete told his father about his aunt's proposal, Jack scratched his head and told him to take the land before his aunt went and donated it to somebody's dog.

End of story. Pete accepted the property and was in the process of figuring out how to give an acre to each of his siblings. He'd thought of building a house here, maybe a big farmhouse with a wraparound porch and wicker chairs. That sounded peaceful and right now, that's what he needed.

But it would mean more to share it with somebody. Oh, hell, he might as well admit the truth. It would mean more to share it with Elissa. He'd heard her name tossed about a few times. Once by Nate, another by Christine, and Pop Benito had mentioned her three or four different times. There'd been a curious look on the old man's face when he said her name, as though waiting for Pete's reaction. No luck there, because Pete knew how to keep his feelings tucked away from everyone.

Except Elissa.

He'd thought of contacting her several times since he'd left the cabin, but he had no idea where she was or how to get in touch with her. They'd never exchanged phone numbers and if the Desantros hadn't mentioned her last name, he still wouldn't know it. But that wasn't why he hadn't tried to get in touch with her and he was a fool to pretend it was. Fear kept him away. Fear that he'd hurt her that last day with his harsh words and accusations and killed whatever she'd felt for him. He still didn't agree with her allegiance to that Blacksworth woman, but he guessed he had to respect her loyalty—however misguided it had been.

The more time he spent with the couples in town like the Desantros, the Reeds, and his aunt's favorites, the Casherdons, the more he understood what compromise really meant. You could love a person and not agree with them all the time, and if you disagreed, it didn't mean you weren't meant to be together. If you shared fundamental principles and values, then you'd make it as a couple. It was work. Damn hard work. But it sure looked like it was worth it.

Pete swiped a hand over his forehead, wished again he had one of the father's ball caps. If Elissa were here, she would have remembered the ball cap...and she'd have an idea or two about what kind of house to build. He pictured her face turning pink with excitement when she talked about it, full lips smiling... There were a lot of women in this town, and quite a few had been obvious about their interest in him. Phone calls, flowers, cakes, and pies. He didn't want any of them.

He wanted Elissa.

So, what the hell was he going to do about it?

A WOMAN COULD ONLY WAIT SO LONG for a man to come after her. Two months was a lifetime, and yet there'd been no word from Pete Finnegan, which could mean just about anything. He really had been pretending in the cabin and had no real feelings for her; he'd had feelings for her, but they'd died when he discovered the notebook... Or, he didn't know how he felt about her and wouldn't know until he saw her again.

She chose to believe the last one.

What else could a woman think when *everything* reminded her of him? Darn it all, she was not going to live the rest of her life waiting for the man to wake up and realize he cared about her, maybe even loved her. Elissa Marie Cerdi was going to take action. No playbooks, no lists or timelines, nothing but her heart and her instincts guiding her.

And they both pointed to Magdalena.

Her parents worried she'd set herself up for serious heartache, worse than the fiasco with Zachary, but what could be worse than the not knowing? The old Elissa would wait and pray, hoping for the day when the man who owned her heart would rescue her from a life of loneliness and despair. The new Elissa said *to heck with that* and decided to rescue herself. One way or another, Pete Finnegan was going to own up to his feelings. One day in late June, Elissa packed her car, kissed her parents good-bye, and took off for Magdalena with a promise to let them know when she arrived and when she'd return. No need to tell them that no matter what happened in Magdalena, her life would not be in Chicago. That conversation would come later, though the extra-tight hug her mother gave her said she might already know.

It was close to dinnertime when she pulled into the Heart Sent, the bed-and-breakfast where she'd booked a room for the next few days. The proprietor was a spry, inquisitive woman with blue eyes and dangly ball earrings. Elissa's plan to keep quiet about her reason for visiting Magdalena spilled out over a dish of Chicken Marsala.

"So...you and Pete Finnegan..."

Elissa nodded. "I had an opportunity to tell him the truth about some things, but I didn't, and when he found out..."

Mimi Pendergrass forked a piece of chicken. "Oh, yes, the Finnegans are big on honesty. I'm sure Pete didn't take it well."

"He didn't, and worse, I tried to defend my reason for not telling him." She bit her bottom lip. "It was a disaster. One minute we were laughing and happy and the next, he was gone."

Mimi reached over, patted Elissa's hand. "He's had enough time to cool off. I'm sure he's regretted his decision more than once, but the Finnegan's are a tough lot; don't like to admit when they're wrong. His father's the same way." She *tsk-tsked* and laughed. "Dolly, that's Jack's wife, deserves a medal and a straight trip to Heaven when the time comes."

Elissa couldn't let Pete take all the blame; she should have been honest with him. "It's not all his fault."

"I'm sure it's not. It takes two to tango, my dear, and I'll be the first to tell you I've known my share of relationship messes." She took a healthy sip of wine, dabbed her lips. "And because of my vast experience in this unfortunate area, I can always tell when somebody's in a fix and hurting." Her blue eyes sparkled and a smile crept over her lips. "Pete's definitely in a fix and hurting. You want to know how I know?" The smile spread. "Women are practically throwing their panties at him to get his attention. And Dolly told me about the phone calls to the house, the notes, the cakes, and pies. Goodness, she said there were some risqué photos, too. Can you imagine?"

Elissa clutched her wine glass, nodded. Any female with a heartbeat would be attracted to the man. "What did he do?" She didn't really want to know, but the not knowing would be worse.

"Do?" Mimi sat back and laughed. "He didn't *do* anything. Dolly said he gave the goodies to his father who took them to the shop and he tossed the letters in the trash—" she paused, tilted her head to the side "—unopened. Yes, he sure did. Dolly only knew about the photos because she thought they were recipe cards and opened them herself." *Tsk-tsk*. "Said they near gave her a heart attack."

"So, what's he been doing?"

"Well, he's been busy, that's for sure. He's helping one of his cousins renovate a house and he's remodeling his aunt's bathroom. She's something else. Edith Finnegan's her name. The woman is one strange canary, but she's always had a soft spot for Pete. Dolly told me she up and gave him the deeds to a big stretch of land, just because. Imagine that?" She shook her head and the dangle ball earrings bounced against her neck. "But Pete, being the honest soul he is, thought it only fair to give his siblings a tract of land. I don't think he chopped it five ways, for the number of kids in the family, but he deserves credit for gifting them anything."

"He plans to stay in Magdalena?" He'd told her he had a lot to figure out and wasn't sure where he'd end up. Sounded like he'd decided on small-town life in his hometown. She could picture him in this place. Hadn't he told her how much he enjoyed improving existing structures, rather than ordering them torn down?

"I'd say he's staying." She slid a look at Elissa, said in a soft voice, "But there are other factors to consider." Mimi shrugged and turned back to her meal. "Guess time will tell, won't it, dear?"

That last comment signaled the end of the conversation about Pete Finnegan and his plans. Mimi changed the subject to gardening, perennial flowers, and The Bleeding Hearts Society, a group of residents interested in beautifying the town and spreading goodwill through flowers and acts of kindness. Apparently, Mimi was part of this group and invited Elissa to attend the next meeting as her guest—if she were still in town.

"We do more than plant flowers and weed beds." She winked and added, "Lots more. Now why don't you head to the sitting room and relax while I clean up the kitchen. Then I'll fix coffee and peach cobbler. The cobbler recipe comes from one of the best bakers in the area. Her name's Ramona and she's on a Mediterranean cruise with her husband. Just got married this past Christmas." Her voice turned soft. "Talk about love taking a long time to find its way. Now go on ahead and check out the reading material in there."

"Are you sure I can't help you clean up the kitchen? It'll be much easier with two people."

"No, no. I can clean it up in a jiff."

"All right, but let me know if you change your mind." Elissa made her way to the sitting room, spotted a photo album on the coffee table labeled *Heart Sent Memories*. She flipped open the first page, studied the attractive couple smiling at one another, so clearly in love. Ben and Gina Reed. The next page revealed another couple, equally attractive, equally engrossed in one another. Roman and Angie Ventori. More pages, more this-is-what-love-looks-like couples. Michael and Elise Androvich, Bree Kinkaid and Adam Brandon. On and on the pages went, a visual testimony to love and happily-ever-after. What about Bree and Adam? They were the only couple who didn't appear to be married. Were they engaged? She'd have to ask Mimi about their story...

"Elissa?"

Pete Finnegan's voice burst through her thoughts, captured her heart. He stood in the entrance of the sitting room, tanned and rugged, wearing a white button-down shirt and jeans, a bouquet of red roses in his arms—more handsome than she remembered. "Pete? What are you doing here?"

He moved toward her, his expression serious, mouth set in a hard line. "Mimi called and told me you were here."

That voice made her stomach do flip-flops. "Mimi?" She glanced toward the back of the house where the proprietor was supposedly tidying up and preparing coffee and peach cobbler. Sounded like she'd taken a detour to make a phone call. "Why would Mimi call you?"

He shrugged, his gaze intense. "Guess she's trying to play matchmaker. I told you this town butts into everybody's business, didn't I?"

Pete had told her a lot of things, some she'd rather forget. "You did mention that. Several times."

"Yeah, sometimes I don't know when to shut up." A dull red washed out the tan in his cheeks, spread to his neck. "I'm going to have to work on that." He cleared his throat, handed her the bouquet of roses. "These are for you. I remember you said red roses were your favorite."

They'd been talking about flowers at the cabin one night and he'd said his aunt grew roses and treated them like her children. "You didn't pick these from your aunt's garden, did you?"

That made him laugh. "I know better than to fool with Aunt Edith's roses. She'd come after me with a shovel if I even thought about it."

"Thank you." Elissa closed her eyes and breathed in their scent. "They're beautiful."

"Yes, they are," he said, his voice husky. "I've got a lot of apologizing to do. I...was hurt and angry. I'm sorry I acted like a jerk, and I'm sorry I took off like I did." He dragged a hand through his hair. "I should have stayed and talked it through, but I'm not used to caring enough to do that. Usually, the explosion comes from the other party and I use it as an excuse to duck out." He sat next to her, clasped her hand, his voice dipping so low she had to lean toward him to hear. "But you were different."

"You aren't the only one with regrets. I should have told you about the notebook and the letters. That's another one of the reasons I came here. I want to apologize to the people I might have hurt." She paused, took a deep breath. "Nate and Christine Desantro, Harry Blacksworth, the MacGregors. Your father."

"I think it's best to let it alone. People don't like their secrets tossed back at them, even if it's in the form of an apology. As for my dad, Nate knows."

Elissa blinked hard, fought back tears. "I wish I'd never sent that letter."

"Dad went to see him right after I called. He said the conversation was long overdue. I'm not sure what happened with the letter, but it didn't matter after that."

"Good." There was so much she wanted to tell him, but a sudden shyness overtook her. They weren't in some hideaway miles from people they knew, pretending nothing existed outside of the cabin walls. A whole town surrounded them with people who'd known Pete Finnegan since he was a boy and others who still cursed Gloria Blacksworth for what she'd tried to do to their friends and family.

"Hey." Pete touched her shoulder. "Why so quiet? What's wrong?"

"Back in the cabin? I wasn't pretending with you, Pete. What I felt was real."

"I know. Me, too."

"But real is scary, and messy."

His lips twitched. "So I've heard."

"You don't even know my last name."

"Cerdi. Elissa Marie Cerdi."

"Who told you?" She narrowed her gaze on him. "You cheated back at the cabin, didn't you? You looked in my wallet." They'd made a pact to use first names and to not go hunting for last names.

"I didn't." He shrugged and said, "I heard it around town. Nate and Christine Desantro mentioned it, and so did Pop Benito."

"Pop Benito?"

"He's the guy they call the Godfather of Magdalena. Big on wisdom, helps people out of their messes." He smiled, added, "The usual stuff." The smile faded. "I didn't care about your last name when we were at the cabin, and I still don't. We knew the important things about each other, and that's all that mattered. But if you want a cheat sheet, I'll be happy to fill one out."

"Are you teasing me?"

The intensity in his gaze burned her. "I've never been more serious. I'll tell you anything you want to know. All you have to do is ask."

The sweetness in those words made her heart swell, her

soul ache. She trailed a hand along his jaw, leaned close, and kissed him. Soft, hesitant. With reverence and love.

"Elissa," he murmured, his hands sliding down her back, pulling her closer.

Oh, but she had missed him. His touch, his voice, his mouth... She put the flowers aside, flung her arms around his neck, deepened the kiss. When she moaned, he pulled back, eyes glittering with need.

"I want you," he said, his voice hoarse. "All of you. Always." Pause. "I love you, Elissa Cerdi."

She stroked his cheek, his chin. "I fell in love with you somewhere between our conversations and your cooking."

He laughed. "Marry me. Let's grow old together."

"Yes," she whispered. "Yes."

He trailed his lips along her neck, her throat, settled a hand on the top button of her shirt. "I think you should show me your room. You know, I'm from this town, but I've never made it upstairs."

She laughed. "Tonight, you will."

"I like the sound of that." His tongue traced a circle behind her ear, made her moan.

"What about Mimi? I think she's fixing coffee and dessert. She's been so nice to me, I'd hate to disappoint her."

Pete eased his hand up her thigh. "I think Mimi already knows what you're having for dessert. In fact, my guess is she planned it."

Elissa pulled back, looked at him. "You mean there's no peach cobbler?"

"There might be." His lips twitched. "And if there is, it'll probably be waiting for us later."

"Later?" she squeaked, not sure she liked having a senior citizen know she planned to take a man to her room, or what she planned to do with him there.

He shrugged, kissed her mouth. "Like I said, this is a town of busybodies, but they mean well. Can you picture yourself living here?" He stumbled over the next words. "Raising a family here?"

She blinked hard to keep the tears from falling, but it was no use. "Absolutely," she whispered. "As long as we're together, that's home."

"I like the sound of that." He swiped at a tear with his finger. "I don't have a lot of money right now, but I've got some land and a few ideas."

"We have each other, Pete. We're already rich." Elissa held his gaze. "Besides, Mrs. Blacksworth left me some money. What better way to use it than to put down roots in Magdalena?"

"From what I've heard about that woman, she wouldn't like that."

"Exactly, but she doesn't control me anymore." The words freed her, made her realize the truth in them. "We can do whatever we want and I want to invest in us. Right here." She kissed him, worked up a smile. "I have an early birthday present for you."

"You do? My birthday's not for another ten months."

"Then it's a really early present." She clasped his hand between hers, kissed his fingers. "I bought the cabin. I couldn't imagine anyone in it but us. It'll be perfect for weekend trips, and teaching kids about the woods and walking trails…"

Pete pulled her to him, held her tight. "I love it. And I love you."

"I love you, too." Pause. "I have another gift for you, too."

"Better than the cabin?"

"Hmm. Maybe." She eased out of his embrace, clasped his face between her hands, kissed him softly on the mouth. "This one's upstairs. Invitation only." One more kiss, and a whisper, "And you're invited."

MANY THANKS for choosing to spend your time reading *A Family Affair: The Cabin*. I'm truly grateful. If you enjoyed it, please consider writing a review on the site where you purchased it. (Short ones are equally welcome.) And now, I must head back to Magdalena and help these characters get in and out of trouble! If you'd like to be notified of my new releases, please sign up at my website: *http://www.marycampisi.com*.

ABOUT THE AUTHOR

Mary Campisi is the bestselling author of over 40 emotion-packed, romantic women's fiction novels that center around hope, redemption, and second chances. Set in small towns, these books take readers through the lives of the characters as they encounter, misfortune, disappointment, and challenges to find hope, friendship and, in some cases, love. Growing up in a small town gives Mary a real sense of how people pull together to help others find their true destiny. Her stories will make you laugh *and* cry, but in the end, you'll feel like you want to live in these towns, meet the residents for coffee or share a meal.

Mary's Truth in Lies series, also known as the *A Family Affair* books, takes place in the Catskill Mountains and centers around the discovery of a man's secret family that prompts the question, *Which family is the real one?* The continued success of this series is driven by readers wanting more and she's created an equally compelling one with the Reunion Gap series.

Mary should have known she'd become a writer when at age thirteen she began changing the ending to all of the books she read. It took several years and a number of jobs, including registered nurse, receptionist in a swanky hair salon, accounts payable clerk, and practice manager in an OB/GYN office, for her to rediscover writing. Enter a mouse-less computer, a floppy disk, and a dream large enough to fill a zip drive. The rest of the story lives on in every book she writes.

When she's not working on her craft or following the lives of five adult children, Mary's digging in the dirt with her flowers and herbs, cooking, reading, walking her rescue lab, Henry, or, on the perfect day, riding off into the sunset with her very own hero/husband on his Ultra Limited aka Harley.

If you would like to be notified when Mary has a new release, please sign up at http://www.marycampisi.com/book/book-release-mailing-list/

To learn more about Mary and her books...

https://www.marycampisi.com
mary@marycampisi.com

facebook.com/marycampisibooks
twitter.com/MaryCampisi
amazon.com/author/marycampisi
bookbub.com/authors/mary-campisi

Made in the USA
Monee, IL
28 April 2026

49136194R00066